SELECTED SHORT STORIES OF

RABINDRANATH TAGORE

selected short stories of
Rabindranath Tagore

maple press

SELECTED SHORT STORIES OF RABINDRANATH TAGORE

Published by

MAPLE PRESS PRIVATE LIMITED
office: A-63, Sector 58, Noida 201301, U.P., India
phone: +91 120 455 3581, 455 3583
email: info@maplepress.co.in
website: www.maplepress.co.in

Reprinted in 2019

ISBN: 978-93-80816-04-3

Contents

1
THE HUNGRY STONES

My kinsman and myself were returning to Calcutta from our Puja trip when we met the man in a train. From his dress and bearing we took him at first for an up-country Mahomedan, but we were puzzled as we heard him talk. He discoursed upon all subjects so confidently that you might think the Disposer of All Things consulted him at all times in all that He did. Hitherto we had been perfectly happy, as we did not know that secret and unheard-of forces were at work, that the Russians had advanced close to us, that the English had deep and secret policies, that confusion among the native chiefs had come to a head. But our newly-acquired friend said with a sly smile: "There happen more things in heaven and earth, Horatio, than are reported in your newspapers." As we had never stirred out of our homes before, the demeanour of the man struck us dumb with wonder. Be the topic ever so trivial, he would quote science, or comment on the Vedas, or repeat quatrains from some Persian poet; and as we had no pretence to a knowledge of science or the Vedas or Persian, our admiration for him went on increasing, and my kinsman, a theosophist, was firmly convinced that our fellow-passenger must have been supernaturally inspired by some strange "magnetism" or "occult power," by an "astral body" or something of that kind. He listened to the tritest saying that fell from the lips of our extraordinary companion with devotional rapture, and secretly took down notes of his conversation. I fancy that the extraordinary man saw this, and was a little pleased with it.

When the train reached the junction, we assembled in the waiting room for the connection. It was then 10 P.M., and as the train, we heard, was likely to be very late, owing to something wrong in the lines, I spread my bed on the table and was about to lie down for a comfortable doze, when the extraordinary person deliberately set about spinning the following yarn. Of course, I could get no sleep that night.

When, owing to a disagreement about some questions of administrative policy, I threw up my post at Junagarh, and entered the service of the Nizam of Hydria, they appointed me at once, as a strong young man, collector of cotton duties at Barich.

Barich is a lovely place. The Susta "chatters over stony ways and babbles on the pebbles," tripping, like a skilful dancing girl, in through the woods below the lonely hills. A flight of 150 steps rises from the river, and above that flight, on the river's brim and at the foot of the hills, there stands a solitary marble palace. Around it there is no habitation of man--the village and the cotton mart of Barich being far off.

About 250 years ago the Emperor Mahmud Shah II had built this lonely palace for his pleasure and luxury. In his days jets of rose-water spurted from its fountains, and on the cold marble floors of its spray-cooled rooms young Persian damsels would sit, their hair dishevelled before bathing, and, splashing their soft naked feet in the clear water of the reservoirs, would sing, to the tune of the guitar, the ghazals of their vineyards.

The fountains play no longer; the songs have ceased; no longer do snow-white feet step gracefully on the snowy marble. It is but the vast and solitary quarters of cess-collectors like us, men oppressed with solitude and deprived of the society of women. Now, Karim Khan, the old clerk of my office, warned me repeatedly not to take up my abode there. "Pass the day there, if you like," said he, "but never stay the night." I passed it off with a light laugh. The servants said that they would work till dark and go away at night. I gave my ready assent. The house had such a bad name that even thieves would not venture near it after dark.

At first the solitude of the deserted palace weighed upon me like a nightmare. I would stay out, and work hard as long as possible, then return home at night jaded and tired, go to bed and fall asleep.

Before a week had passed, the place began to exert a weird fascination upon me. It is difficult to describe or to induce people to believe; but I felt as if the whole house was like a living organism slowly and imperceptibly digesting me by the action of some stupefying gastric juice.

Perhaps the process had begun as soon as I set my foot in the house, but I distinctly remember the day on which I first was conscious of it.

It was the beginning of summer, and the market being dull I had no work to do. A little before sunset I was sitting in an arm-chair near the water's edge below the steps. The Susta had shrunk and sunk low; a broad patch of sand on the other side glowed with the hues of evening; on this side the pebbles at the bottom of the clear shallow waters were glistening. There was not a breath of wind anywhere, and the still air was laden with an oppressive scent from the spicy shrubs growing on the hills close by.

As the sun sank behind the hill-tops a long dark curtain fell upon the stage of day, and the intervening hills cut short the time in which light and shade mingle at sunset. I thought of going out for a ride, and was about to get up when I heard a footfall on the steps behind. I looked back, but there was no one.

As I sat down again, thinking it to be an illusion, I heard many footfalls, as if a large number of persons were rushing down the steps. A strange thrill of delight, slightly tinged with fear, passed through my frame, and though there was not a figure before my eyes, methought I saw a bevy of joyous maidens coming down the steps to bathe in the Susta in that summer evening. Not a sound was in the valley, in the river, or in the palace, to break the silence, but I distinctly heard the maidens' gay and mirthful laugh, like the gurgle of a spring gushing forth in a hundred cascades, as they ran past me, in quick playful pursuit of each other, towards the river, without noticing me at all. As they were invisible to me, so I was, as it were, invisible to them. The river was perfectly calm, but I felt that its still, shallow, and clear waters were stirred suddenly by the splash of many an arm jingling with bracelets, that the girls laughed and dashed and spattered water at one another, that the feet of the fair swimmers tossed the tiny waves up in showers of pearl.

I felt a thrill at my heart--I cannot say whether the excitement was due to fear or delight or curiosity. I had a strong desire to see them more clearly, but naught was visible before me; I thought I could catch all that they said if I only strained my ears; but however hard I strained them, I heard nothing but the chirping of the cicadas in the woods. It seemed as if a dark curtain of 250 years was hanging before me, and I would fain lift a corner of it tremblingly and peer through, though the assembly on the other side was completely enveloped in darkness.

The oppressive closeness of the evening was broken by a sudden gust of wind, and the still surface of the Suista rippled and curled like the hair of a nymph, and from the woods wrapt in the evening gloom there came forth a simultaneous murmur, as though they were awakening from a black dream. Call it reality or dream, the momentary glimpse of that invisible mirage reflected from a far-off world, 250 years old, vanished in a flash. The mystic forms that brushed past me with their quick unbodied steps, and loud, voiceless laughter, and threw themselves into the river, did not go back wringing their dripping robes as they went. Like fragrance wafted away by the wind they were dispersed by a single breath of the spring.

Then I was filled with a lively fear that it was the Muse that had taken advantage of my solitude and possessed me--the witch had evidently come to ruin a poor devil like myself making a living by collecting cotton duties. I decided to have a good dinner--it is the empty stomach that all sorts of incurable diseases find an easy prey. I sent for my cook and gave orders for a rich, sumptuous moghlai dinner, redolent of spices and ghi.

Next morning the whole affair appeared a queer fantasy. With a light heart I put on a sola hat like the sahebs, and drove out to my work. I was to have written my quarterly report that day, and expected to return late; but before it was dark I was strangely drawn to my house--by what I could not say--I felt they were all waiting, and that I should delay no longer. Leaving my report unfinished I rose, put on my sola hat, and startling the dark, shady, desolate path with the rattle of my carriage, I reached the vast silent palace standing on the gloomy skirts of the hills.

On the first floor the stairs led to a very spacious hall, its roof stretching wide over ornamental arches resting on three rows of massive pillars, and groaning day and night under the weight of its own intense solitude. The day had just closed, and the lamps had not yet been lighted. As I pushed the door open a great bustle seemed to follow within, as if a throng of people had broken up in confusion, and rushed out through the doors and windows and corridors and verandas and rooms, to make its hurried escape.

As I saw no one I stood bewildered, my hair on end in a kind of ecstatic delight, and a faint scent of attar and unguents almost effected by age lingered in my nostrils. Standing in the darkness of that vast desolate hall between the rows of those ancient pillars, I could hear the gurgle of fountains plashing on the marble floor, a strange tune on the guitar, the jingle of ornaments and the tinkle of anklets, the clang of bells tolling the hours, the distant note of nahabat, the din of the crystal pendants of chandeliers shaken by the breeze, the song of bulbuls from the cages in the corridors, the cackle of storks in the gardens, all creating round me a strange unearthly music.

Then I came under such a spell that this intangible, inaccessible, unearthly vision appeared to be the only reality in the world--and all else a mere dream. That I, that is to say, Srijut So-and-so, the eldest son of So-and-so of blessed memory, should be drawing a monthly salary of Rs. 450 by the discharge of my duties as collector of cotton duties, and driving in my dog-cart to my office every day in a short coat and soia hat, appeared to me to be such an astonishingly ludicrous illusion that I burst into a horse-laugh, as I stood in the gloom of that vast silent hall.

At that moment my servant entered with a lighted kerosene lamp in his hand. I do not know whether he thought me mad, but it came back to me at once that I was in very deed Srijut So-and-so, son of So-and-so of blessed memory, and that, while our poets, great and small, alone could say whether inside of or outside the earth there was a region where unseen fountains perpetually played and fairy guitars, struck by invisible fingers, sent forth an eternal harmony, this at any rate was certain, that I collected duties at the cotton market at Banch, and earned thereby Rs. 450 per mensem as my salary. I laughed in great glee at my curious illusion, as I sat over the newspaper at my camp-table, lighted by the kerosene lamp.

After I had finished my paper and eaten my moghlai dinner, I put out the lamp, and lay down on my bed in a small side-room. Through the open window a radiant star, high above the Avalli hills skirted by the darkness of their woods, was gazing intently from millions and millions of miles away in the sky at Mr. Collector lying on a humble camp-bedstead. I wondered and felt amused at the idea, and do not knew when I fell asleep or how long I slept; but I suddenly awoke with a start, though I heard no sound and saw no intruder--only the steady bright star on the hilltop had set, and the dim light of the new moon was stealthily entering the room through the open window, as if ashamed of its intrusion.

I saw nobody, but felt as if some one was gently pushing me. As I awoke she said not a word, but beckoned me with her five fingers bedecked with rings to follow her cautiously. I got up noiselessly, and, though not a soul save myself was there in the countless apartments of that deserted palace with its slumbering sounds and waiting echoes, I feared at every step lest any one should wake up. Most of the rooms of the palace were always kept closed, and I had never entered them.

I followed breathless and with silent steps my invisible guide--I cannot now say where. What endless dark and narrow passages, what long corridors, what silent and solemn audience-chambers and close secret cells I crossed!

Though I could not see my fair guide, her form was not invisible to my mind's eye,--an Arab girl, her arms, hard and smooth as marble, visible through her loose sleeves, a thin veil falling on her face from the fringe of her cap, and a curved dagger at her waist! Methought that one of the thousand and one Arabian Nights had been wafted to me from the world of romance, and that at the dead of night I was wending my way through the dark narrow alleys of slumbering Bagdad to a trysting-place fraught with peril.

At last my fair guide stopped abruptly before a deep blue screen, and seemed to point to something below. There was nothing there, but a sudden dread froze the blood in my heart-methought I saw there on the floor at the foot of the screen a terrible negro eunuch dressed in rich brocade, sitting and dozing with outstretched legs, with a naked sword on his lap. My fair guide lightly tripped over his legs and held up a fringe of the screen. I could catch a glimpse of a part of the room spread with a Persian carpet--some one was sitting inside on a bed--I could not see her, but only caught a glimpse of two exquisite feet in gold-embroidered slippers, hanging out from loose saffron-coloured paijamas and placed idly on the orange-coloured velvet carpet. On one side there was a bluish crystal tray on which a few apples, pears, oranges, and bunches of grapes in plenty, two small cups and a gold-tinted decanter were evidently waiting the guest. A fragrant intoxicating vapour, issuing from a strange sort of incense that burned within, almost overpowered my senses.

As with trembling heart I made an attempt to step across the outstretched legs of the eunuch, he woke up suddenly with a start, and the sword fell from his lap with a sharp clang on the marble floor. A terrific scream made me jump, and I saw I was sitting on that camp-bedstead of mine sweating heavily; and the crescent moon looked pale in the morning light like a weary sleepless patient at dawn; and our crazy Meher Ali was crying out, as is his daily custom, "Stand back! Stand back!!" while he went along the lonely road.

Such was the abrupt close of one of my Arabian Nights; but there were yet a thousand nights left.

Then followed a great discord between my days and nights. During the day I would go to my work worn and tired, cursing the bewitching night and her empty dreams, but as night came my daily life with its bonds and shackles of work would appear a petty, false, ludicrous vanity.

After nightfall I was caught and overwhelmed in the snare of a strange intoxication, I would then be transformed into some unknown personage of a bygone age, playing my part in unwritten history; and my short English coat and tight breeches did not suit me in the least. With a red velvet cap on my head, loose paijamas, an embroidered vest, a long flowing silk gown, and coloured handkerchiefs scented with attar, I would complete my elaborate toilet, sit on a high-cushioned chair, and replace my cigarette with a many-coiled narghileh filled with rose-water, as if in eager expectation of a strange meeting with the beloved one.

I have no power to describe the marvellous incidents that unfolded themselves, as the gloom of the night deepened. I felt as if in the curious apartments of that vast edifice the fragments of a beautiful story, which I could follow for some distance, but of which I could never see the end, flew about in a sudden gust of the vernal breeze. And all the same I would wander from room to room in pursuit of them the whole night long.

Amid the eddy of these dream-fragments, amid the smell of henna and the twanging of the guitar, amid the waves of air charged with fragrant spray, I would catch like a flash of lightning the momentary glimpse of a fair damsel. She it was who had saffron-coloured paijamas, white ruddy soft feet in gold-embroidered slippers with curved toes, a close-fitting bodice wrought with gold, a red cap, from which a golden frill fell on her snowy brow and cheeks.

She had maddened me. In pursuit of her I wandered from room to room, from path to path among the bewildering maze of alleys in the enchanted dreamland of the nether world of sleep.

Sometimes in the evening, while arraying myself carefully as a prince of the blood-royal before a large mirror, with a candle burning on either side, I would see a sudden reflection of the Persian beauty by the side of my own. A swift turn of her neck, a quick eager glance of intense passion and pain glowing in her large dark eyes, just a suspicion of speech on her dainty red lips, her figure, fair and slim crowned with youth like a blossoming creeper, quickly uplifted in her graceful tilting gait, a dazzling flash of pain and craving and ecstasy, a smile and a glance and a blaze of jewels and silk, and she melted away. A wild glist of wind, laden with all the fragrance of hills and woods, would put out my light, and I would fling aside my dress and lie down on my bed, my eyes closed and my body thrilling with delight, and there around me in the breeze, amid all the perfume of the woods and hills, floated through the silent gloom many a caress and many a kiss and many a tender touch of hands, and gentle murmurs in my ears, and fragrant breaths on my brow; or a sweetly-perfumed kerchief was wafted again and again on my cheeks. Then slowly a mysterious serpent would twist her stupefying coils about me; and heaving a heavy sigh, I would lapse into insensibility, and then into a profound slumber.

One evening I decided to go out on my horse--I do not know who implored me to stay-but I would listen to no entreaties that day. My English hat and coat were resting on a rack, and I was about to take them down when a sudden whirlwind, crested with the sands of the Susta and the dead leaves of the Avalli hills, caught them up, and whirled them round and round, while a loud peal of merry laughter rose higher and higher, striking all the chords of mirth till it died away in the land of sunset.

I could not go out for my ride, and the next day I gave up my queer English coat and hat for good.

That day again at dead of night I heard the stifled heart-breaking sobs of some one--as if below the bed, below the floor, below the stony foundation of that gigantic palace, from the depths of a dark damp grave, a voice piteously cried and implored me: "Oh, rescue me! Break through these doors of hard illusion, deathlike slumber and fruitless dreams, place by your side on the saddle, press me to your heart, and, riding through hills and woods and across the river, take me to the warm radiance of your sunny rooms above!"

Who am I? Oh, how can I rescue thee? What drowning beauty, what incarnate passion shall I drag to the shore from this wild eddy of dreams? O lovely ethereal apparition! Where didst thou flourish and when? By what cool spring, under the shade of what date-groves, wast thou born--in the lap of what homeless wanderer in the desert? What Bedouin snatched thee from thy mother's arms, an opening bud plucked from a wild creeper, placed thee on a horse swift as lightning, crossed the burning sands, and took thee to the slave-market of what royal city? And there, what officer of the Badshah, seeing the glory of thy bashful blossoming youth, paid for thee in gold, placed thee in a golden palanquin, and offered thee as a present for the seraglio of his master? And O, the history of that place! The music of the sareng, the jingle of anklets, the occasional flash of daggers and the glowing wine of Shiraz poison, and the piercing flashing glance! What infinite grandeur, what endless servitude!

The slave-girls to thy right and left waved the chamar as diamonds flashed from their bracelets; the Badshah, the king of kings, fell on his knees at thy snowy feet in bejewelled shoes, and outside the terrible Abyssinian eunuch, looking like a messenger of death, but clothed like an angel, stood with a naked sword in his hand! Then, O, thou flower of the desert, swept away by the blood-stained dazzling ocean of grandeur, with its foam of jealousy, its rocks and shoals of intrigue, on what shore of cruel death wast thou cast, or in what other land more splendid and more cruel?

Suddenly at this moment that crazy Meher Ali screamed out: "Stand back! Stand back!! All is false! All is false!!" I opened my eyes and saw that it was already light. My chaprasi came and handed me my letters, and the cook waited with a salam for my orders.

I said; "No, I can stay here no longer." That very day I packed up, and moved to my office. Old Karim Khan smiled a little as he saw me. I felt nettled, but said nothing, and fell to my work.

As evening approached I grew absent-minded; I felt as if I had an appointment to keep; and the work of examining the cotton accounts seemed wholly useless; even the Nizamat of the Nizam did not appear to be of much worth. Whatever belonged to the present, whatever was moving and acting and working for bread seemed trivial, meaningless, and contemptible.

I threw my pen down, closed my ledgers, got into my dog-cart, and drove away. I noticed that it stopped of itself at the gate of the marble palace just at the hour of twilight. With quick steps I climbed the stairs, and entered the room.

A heavy silence was reigning within. The dark rooms were looking sullen as if they had taken offence. My heart was full of contrition, but there was no one to whom I could lay it bare, or of whom I could ask forgiveness. I wandered about the dark rooms with a vacant mind. I wished I had a guitar to which I could sing to the unknown: "O fire, the poor moth that made a vain effort to fly away has come back to thee! Forgive it but this once, burn its wings and consume it in thy flame!"

Suddenly two tear-drops fell from overhead on my brow. Dark masses of clouds overcast the top of the Avalli hills that day. The gloomy woods and the sooty waters of the Susta were waiting in terrible suspense and in an ominous calm. Suddenly land, water, and sky shivered, and a wild tempest-blast rushed howling through the distant pathless woods, showing its lightning-teeth like a raving maniac who had broken his chains. The desolate halls of the palace banged their doors, and moaned in the bitterness of anguish.

The servants were all in the office, and there was no one to light the lamps. The night was cloudy and moonless. In the dense gloom within I could distinctly feel that a woman was lying on her face on the carpet below the bed--clasping and tearing her long dishevelled hair with desperate fingers. Blood was tricking down her fair brow, and she was now laughing a hard, harsh, mirthless laugh, now bursting into violent wringing sobs, now rending her bodice and striking at her bare bosom, as the wind roared in through the open window, and the rain poured in torrents and soaked her through and through.

All night there was no cessation of the storm or of the passionate cry. I wandered from room to room in the dark, with unavailing sorrow. Whom could I console when no one was by? Whose was this intense agony of sorrow? Whence arose this inconsolable grief?

And the mad man cried out: "Stand back! Stand back!! All is false! All is false!!"

I saw that the day had dawned, and Meher Ali was going round and round the palace with his usual cry in that dreadful weather. Suddenly it came to me that perhaps he also had once lived in that house, and that, though he had gone mad, he came there every day, and went round and round, fascinated by the weird spell cast by the marble demon.

Despite the storm and rain I ran to him and asked: "Ho, Meher Ali, what is false?"

The man answered nothing, but pushing me aside went round and round with his frantic cry, like a bird flying fascinated about the jaws of a snake, and made a desperate effort to warn himself by repeating: "Stand back! Stand back!! All is false! All is false!!"

I ran like a mad man through the pelting rain to my office, and asked Karim Khan: "Tell me the meaning of all this!"

What I gathered from that old man was this: That at one time countless unrequited passions and unsatisfied longings and lurid flames of wild blazing pleasure raged within that palace, and that the curse of all the heart-aches and blasted hopes had made its every stone thirsty and hungry, eager to swallow up like a famished ogress any living man who might chance to approach. Not one of those who lived there for three consecutive nights could escape these cruel jaws, save Meher Ali, who had escaped at the cost of his reason.

I asked: "Is there no means whatever of my release?" The old man said: "There is only one means, and that is very difficult. I will tell you what it is, but first you must hear the history of a young Persian girl who once lived in that pleasure-dome. A stranger or a more bitterly heart-rending tragedy was never enacted on this earth."

Just at this moment the coolies announced that the train was coming. So soon? We hurriedly packed up our luggage, as the tram steamed in. An English gentleman, apparently just aroused from slumber, was looking out of a first-class carriage endeavouring to read the name of the station. As soon as he caught sight of our fellow-passenger, he cried, "Hallo," and took him into his own compartment. As we got into a second-class carriage, we had no chance of finding out who the man was nor what was the end of his story.

I said; "The man evidently took us for fools and imposed upon us out of fun. The story is pure fabrication from start to finish." The discussion that followed ended in a lifelong rupture between my theosophist kinsman and myself.

2

THE VICTORY

She was the Princess Ajita. And the court poet of King Narayan had never seen her. On the day he recited a new poem to the king he would raise his voice just to that pitch which could be heard by unseen hearers in the screened balcony high above the hall. He sent up his song towards the star-land out of his reach, where, circled with light, the planet who ruled his destiny shone unknown and out of ken.

He would espy some shadow moving behind the veil. A tinkling sound would come to his ear from afar, and would set him dreaming of the ankles whose tiny golden bells sang at each step. Ah, the rosy red tender feet that walked the dust of the earth like God's mercy on the fallen! The poet had placed them on the altar of his heart, where he wove his songs to the tune of those golden bells. Doubt never arose in his mind as to whose shadow it was that moved behind the screen, and whose anklets they were that sang to the time of his beating heart.

Manjari, the maid of the princess, passed by the poet's house on her way to the river, and she never missed a day to have a few words with him on the sly. When she found the road deserted, and the shadow of dusk on the land, she would boldly enter his room, and sit at the corner of his carpet. There was a suspicion of an added care in the choice of the colour of her veil, in the setting of the flower in her hair.

People smiled and whispered at this, and they were not to blame. For Shekhar the poet never took the trouble to hide the fact that these meetings were a pure joy to him.

The meaning of her name was the spray of flowers. One must confess that for an ordinary mortal it was sufficient in its sweetness. But Shekhar made his own addition to this name, and called her the Spray of Spring Flowers. And ordinary mortals shook their heads and said, Ah, me!

In the spring songs that the poet sang the praise of the spray of spring flowers was conspicuously reiterated; and the king winked and smiled at him when he heard it, and the poet smiled in answer.

The king would put him the question; "Is it the business of the bee merely to hum in the court of the spring?"

The poet would answer; "No, but also to sip the honey of the spray of spring flowers."

And they all laughed in the king's hall. And it was rumoured that the Princess Akita also laughed at her maid's accepting the poet's name for her, and Manjari felt glad in her heart.

Thus truth and falsehood mingle in life--and to what God builds man adds his own decoration.

Only those were pure truths which were sung by the poet. The theme was Krishna, the lover god, and Radha, the beloved, the Eternal Man and the Eternal Woman, the sorrow that comes from the beginning of time, and the joy without end. The truth of these songs was tested in his inmost heart by everybody from the beggar to the king himself. The poet's songs were on the lips of all. At the merest glimmer of the moon and the faintest whisper of the summer breeze his songs would break forth in the land from windows and courtyards, from sailing-boats, from shadows of the wayside trees, in numberless voices.

Thus passed the days happily. The poet recited, the king listened, the hearers applauded, Manjari passed and repassed by the poet's room on her way to the river--the shadow flitted behind the screened balcony, and the tiny golden bells tinkled from afar.

Just then set forth from his home in the south a poet on his path of conquest. He came to King Narayan, in the kingdom of Amarapur. He stood before the throne, and uttered a verse in praise of the king. He had challenged all the court poets on his way, and his career of victory had been unbroken.

The king received him with honour, and said: "Poet, I offer you welcome."

Pundarik, the poet, proudly replied: "Sire, I ask for war."

Shekhar, the court poet of the king did not know how the battle of the muse was to be waged. He had no sleep at night. The mighty figure of the famous Pundarik, his sharp nose curved like a scimitar, and his proud head tilted on one side, haunted the poet's vision in the dark.

With a trembling heart Shekhar entered the arena in the morning. The theatre was filled with the crowd.

The poet greeted his rival with a smile and a bow. Pundarik returned it with a slight toss of his head, and turned his face towards his circle of adoring followers with a meaning smile. Shekhar cast his glance towards the screened balcony high above, and saluted his lady in his mind, saying! "If I am the winner at the combat to-day, my lady, thy victorious name shall be glorified."

The trumpet sounded. The great crowd stood up, shouting victory to the king. The king, dressed in an ample robe of white, slowly came into the hall like a floating cloud of autumn, and sat on his throne.

Pundarik stood up, and the vast hall became still. With his head raised high and chest expanded, he began in his thundering voice to recite the praise of King Narayan. His words burst upon the walls of the hall like breakers of the sea, and seemed to rattle against the ribs of the listening crowd. The skill with which he gave varied meanings to the name Narayan, and wove each letter of it through the web of his verses in all mariner of combinations, took away the breath of his amazed hearers.

For some minutes after he took his seat his voice continued to vibrate among the numberless pillars of the king's court and in thousands of speechless hearts. The learned professors who had come from distant lands raised their right hands, and cried, Bravo!

The king threw a glance on Shekhar's face, and Shekhar in answer raised for a moment his eyes full of pain towards his master, and then stood up like a stricken deer at bay. His face was pale, his bashfulness was almost that of a woman, his slight youthful figure, delicate in its outline, seemed like a tensely strung vina ready to break out in music at the least touch.

His head was bent, his voice was low, when he began. The first few verses were almost inaudible. Then he slowly raised his head, and his clear sweet voice rose into the sky like a quivering flame of fire. He began with the ancient legend of the kingly line lost in the haze of the past, and brought it down through its long course of heroism and matchless generosity to the present age. He fixed his gaze on the king's face, and all the vast and unexpressed love of the people for the royal house rose like incense in his song, and enwreathed the throne on all sides. These were his last words when, trembling, he took his seat: "My master, I may be beaten in play of words, but not in my love for thee."

Tears filled the eyes of the hearers, and the stone walls shook with cries of victory.

Mocking this popular outburst of feeling, with an august shake of his head and a contemptuous sneer, Pundarik stood up, and flung this question to the assembly; "What is there superior to words?" In a moment the hall lapsed into silence again.

Then with a marvellous display of learning, he proved that the Word was in the beginning, that the Word was God. He piled up quotations from scriptures, and built a high altar for the Word to be seated above all that there is in heaven and in earth. He repeated that question in his mighty voice: "What is there superior to words?"

Proudly he looked around him. None dared to accept his challenge, and he slowly took his seat like a lion who had just made a full meal of its victim. The pandits shouted, Bravo! The king remained silent with wonder, and the poet Shekhar felt himself of no account by the side of this stupendous learning. The assembly broke up for that day.

Next day Shekhar began his song. It was of that day when the pipings of love's flute startled for the first time the hushed air of the Vrinda forest. The shepherd women did not know who was the player or whence came the music. Sometimes it seemed to come from the heart of the south wind, and sometimes from the straying clouds of the hilltops. It came with a message of tryst from the land of the sunrise, and it floated from the verge of sunset with its sigh of sorrow. The stars seemed to be the stops of the instrument that flooded the dreams of the night with melody. The music seemed to burst all at once from all sides, from fields and groves, from the shady lanes and lonely roads, from the melting blue of the sky, from the shimmering green of the grass. They neither knew its meaning nor could they find words to give utterance to the desire of their hearts. Tears filled their eyes, and their life seemed to long for a death that would be its consummation.

Shekhar forgot his audience, forgot the trial of his strength with a rival. He stood alone amid his thoughts that rustled and quivered round him like leaves in a summer breeze, and sang the Song of the Flute. He had in his mind the vision of an image that had taken its shape from a shadow, and the echo of a faint tinkling sound of a distant footstep.

He took his seat. His hearers trembled with the sadness of an indefinable delight, immense and vague, and they forgot to applaud him. As this feeling died away Pundarik stood up before the throne and challenged his rival to define who was this Lover and who was the Beloved. He arrogantly looked around him, he smiled at his followers and then put the question again: "Who is Krishna, the lover, and who is Radha, the beloved?"

Then he began to analyse the roots of those names,--and various interpretations of their meanings. He brought before the bewildered audience all the intricacies of the different schools of metaphysics with consummate skill. Each letter of those names he divided from its fellow, and then pursued them with a relentless logic till they fell to the dust in confusion, to be caught up again and restored to a meaning never before imagined by the subtlest of word-mongers.

The pandits were in ecstasy; they applauded vociferously; and the crowd followed them, deluded into the certainty that they had witnessed, that day, the last shred of the curtains of Truth torn to pieces before their eyes by a prodigy of intellect. The performance of his tremendous feat so delighted them that they forgot to ask themselves if there was any truth behind it after all.

The king's mind was overwhelmed with wonder. The atmosphere was completely cleared of all illusion of music, and the vision of the world around seemed to be changed from its freshness of tender green to the solidity of a high road levelled and made hard with crushed stones.

To the people assembled their own poet appeared a mere boy in comparison with this giant, who walked with such case, knocking down difficulties at each step in the world of words and thoughts. It became evident to them for the first time that the poems Shekhar wrote were absurdly simple, and it must be a mere accident that they did not write them themselves. They were neither new, nor difficult, nor instructive, nor necessary.

The king tried to goad his poet with keen glances, silently inciting him to make a final effort. But Shekhar took no notice, and remained fixed to his seat.

The king in anger came down from his throne--took off his pearl chain and put it on Pundarik's head. Everybody in the hall cheered. From the upper balcony came a slight sound of the movements of rustling robes and waist-chains hung with golden bells. Shekhar rose from his seat and left the hall.

It was a dark night of waning moon. The poet Shekhar took down his MSS. from his shelves and heaped them on the floor. Some of them contained his earliest writings, which he had almost forgotten. He turned over the pages, reading passages here and there. They all seemed to him poor and trivial--mere words and childish rhymes!

One by one he tore his books to fragments, and threw them into a vessel containing fire, and said: "To thee, to thee, O my beauty, my fire! Thou hast been burning in my heart all these futile years. If my life were a piece of gold it would come out of its trial brighter, but it is a trodden turf of grass, and nothing remains of it but this handful of ashes."

The night wore on. Shekhar opened wide his windows. He spread upon his bed the white flowers that he loved, the jasmines, tuberoses and chrysanthemums, and brought into his bedroom all the lamps he had in his house and lighted them. Then mixing with honey the juice of some poisonous root he drank it and lay down on his bed.

Golden anklets tinkled in the passage outside the door, and a subtle perfume came into the room with the breeze.

The poet, with his eyes shut, said; "My lady, have you taken pity upon your servant at last and come to see him?"

The answer came in a sweet voice "My poet, I have come."

Shekhar opened his eyes--and saw before his bed the figure of a woman.

His sight was dim and blurred. And it seemed to him that the image made of a shadow that he had ever kept throned in the secret shrine of his heart had come into the outer world in his last moment to gaze upon his face.

The woman said; "I am the Princess Ajita."

The poet with a great effort sat up on his bed.

The princess whispered into his car: "The king has not done you justice. It was you who won at the combat, my poet, and I have come to crown you with the crown of victory."

She took the garland of flowers from her own neck, and put it on his hair, and the poet fell down upon his bed stricken by death.

3
ONCE THERE WAS A KING

"Once upon a time there was a king."

When we were children there was no need to know who the king in the fairy story was. It didn't matter whether he was called Shiladitya or Shaliban, whether he lived at Kashi or Kanauj. The thing that made a seven-year-old boy's heart go thump, thump with delight was this one sovereign truth; this reality of all realities: "Once there was a king."

But the readers of this modern age are far more exact and exacting. When they hear such an opening to a story, they are at once critical and suspicious. They apply the searchlight of science to its legendary haze and ask: "Which king?"

The story-tellers have become more precise in their turn. They are no longer content with the old indefinite, "There was a king," but assume instead a look of profound learning, and begin: "Once there was a king named Ajatasatru,"

The modern reader's curiosity, however, is not so easily satisfied. He blinks at the author through his scientific spectacles, and asks again: "Which Ajatasatru?"

"Every schoolboy knows," the author proceeds, "that there were three Ajatasatrus. The first was born in the twentieth century B.C., and died at the tender age of two years and eight months, I deeply regret that it is impossible to find, from any trustworthy source, a detailed account of his reign. The second Ajatasatru is better known to historians. If you refer to the new Encyclopedia of History...."

By this time the modern reader's suspicions are dissolved. He feels he may safely trust his author. He says to himself: "Now we shall have a story that is both improving and instructive."

Ah! how we all love to be deluded! We have a secret dread of being thought ignorant. And we end by being ignorant after all, only we have done it in a long and roundabout way.

There is an English proverb; "Ask me no questions, and I will tell you no lies." The boy of seven who is listening to a fairy story understands that perfectly well; he withholds his questions, while the story is being told. So the pure and beautiful falsehood of it all remains naked and innocent as a babe; transparent as truth itself; limpid as afresh bubbling spring. But the ponderous and learned lie of our moderns has to keep its true character draped and veiled. And if there is discovered anywhere the least little peep-hole of deception, the reader turns away with a prudish disgust, and the author is discredited.

When we were young, we understood all sweet things; and we could detect the sweets of a fairy story by an unerring science of our own. We never cared for such useless things as knowledge. We only cared for truth. And our unsophisticated little hearts knew well where the Crystal Palace of Truth lay and how to reach it. But to-day we are expected to write pages of facts, while the truth is simply this:

"There was a king."

I remember vividly that evening in Calcutta when the fairy story began. The rain and the storm had been incessant. The whole of the city was flooded. The water was knee-deep in our lane. I had a straining hope, which was almost a certainty, that my tutor would be prevented from coming that evening. I sat on the stool in the far corner of the veranda looking down the lane, with a heart beating faster and faster. Every minute I kept my eye on the rain, and when it began to grow less I prayed with all my might; "Please, God, send some more rain till half-past seven is over." For I was quite ready to believe that there was no other need for rain except to protect one helpless boy one evening in one corner of Calcutta from the deadly clutches of his tutor.

If not in answer to my prayer, at any rate according to some grosser law of physical nature, the rain did not give up.

But, alas! nor did my teacher.

Exactly to the minute, in the bend of the lane, I saw his approaching umbrella. The great bubble of hope burst in my breast, and my heart collapsed. Truly, if there is a punishment to fit the crime after death, then my tutor will be born again as me, and I shall be born as my tutor.

As soon as I saw his umbrella I ran as hard as I could to my mother's room. My mother and my grandmother were sitting opposite one another playing cards by the light of a lamp. I ran into the room, and flung myself on the bed beside my mother, and said:

"Mother dear, the tutor has come, and I have such a bad headache; couldn't I have no lessons today?"

I hope no child of immature age will be allowed to read this story, and I sincerely trust it will not be used in text-books or primers for schools. For what I did was dreadfully bad, and I received no punishment whatever. On the contrary, my wickedness was crowned with success.

My mother said to me: "All right," and turning to the servant added: "Tell the tutor that he can go back home."

It was perfectly plain that she didn't think my illness very serious, as she went on with her game as before, and took no further notice. And I also, burying my head in the pillow, laughed to my heart's content. We perfectly understood one another, my mother and I.

But every one must know how hard it is for a boy of seven years old to keep up the illusion of illness for a long time. After about a minute I got hold of Grandmother, and said: "Grannie, do tell me a story."

I had to ask this many times. Grannie and Mother went on playing cards, and took no notice. At last Mother said to me: "Child, don't bother. Wait till we've finished our game." But I persisted: "Grannie, do tell me a story." I told Mother she could finish her game to-morrow, but she must let Grannie tell me a story there and then.

At last Mother threw down the cards and said: "You had better do what he wants. I can't manage him." Perhaps she had it in her mind that she would have no tiresome tutor on the morrow, while I should be obliged to be back to those stupid lessons.

As soon as ever Mother had given way, I rushed at Grannie. I got hold of her hand, and, dancing with delight, dragged her inside my mosquito curtain on to the bed. I clutched hold of the bolster with both hands in my excitement, and jumped up and down with joy, and when I had got a little quieter, said: "Now, Grannie, let' s have the story!"

Grannie went on: "And the king had a queen." That was good to begin with. He had only one.

It is usual for kings in fairy stories to be extravagant in queens. And whenever we hear that there are two queens, our hearts begin to sink. One is sure to be unhappy. But in Grannie's story that danger was past. He had only one queen.

We next hear that the king had not got any son. At the age of seven I didn't think there was any need to bother if a man had had no son. He might only have been in the way. Nor are we greatly excited when we hear that the king has gone away into the forest to practise austerities in order to get a son. There was only one thing that would have made me go into the forest, and that was to get away from my tutor!

But the king left behind with his queen a small girl, who grew up into a beautiful princess.

Twelve years pass away, and the king goes on practising austerities, and never thinks all this while of his beautiful daughter. The princess has reached the full bloom of her youth. The age of marriage has passed, but the king does not return. And the queen pines away with grief and cries: "Is my golden daughter destined to die unmarried? Ah me! What a fate is mine."

Then the queen sent men to the king to entreat him earnestly to come back for a single night and take one meal in the palace. And the king consented.

The queen cooked with her own hand, and with the greatest care, sixty-four dishes, and made a seat for him of sandal-wood, and arranged the food in plates of gold and cups of silver. The princess stood behind with the peacock-tail fan in her hand. The king, after twelve years' absence, came into the house, and the princess waved the fan, lighting up all the room with her beauty. The king looked in his daughter's face, and forgot to take his food.

At last he asked his queen: "Pray, who is this girl whose beauty shines as the gold image of the goddess? Whose daughter is she?"

The queen beat her forehead, and cried: "Ah, how evil is my fate! Do you not know your own daughter?"

The king was struck with amazement. He said at last; "My tiny daughter has grown to be a woman."

"What else?" the queen said with a sigh. "Do you not know that twelve years have passed by?"

"But why did you not give her in marriage?" asked the king.

"You were away," the queen said. "And how could I find her a suitable husband?"

The king became vehement with excitement. "The first man I see to-morrow," he said, "when I come out of the palace shall marry her."

The princess went on waving her fan of peacock feathers, and the king finished his meal.

The next morning, as the king came out of his palace, he saw the son of a Brahman gathering sticks in the forest outside the palace gates. His age was about seven or eight.

The king said: "I will marry my daughter to him."

Who can interfere with a king's command? At once the boy was called, and the marriage garlands were exchanged between him and the princess. At this point I came up close to my wise Grannie and asked her eagerly: "What then?"

In the bottom of my heart there was a devout wish to substitute myself for that fortunate wood-gatherer of seven years old. The night was resonant with the patter of rain. The earthen lamp by my bedside was burning low. My grandmother's voice droned on as she told the story. And all these things served to create in a corner of my credulous heart the belief that I had been gathering sticks in the dawn of some indefinite time in the kingdom of some unknown king, and in a moment garlands had been exchanged between me and the princess, beautiful as the Goddess of Grace. She had a gold band on her hair and gold earrings in her ears. She bad a necklace and bracelets of gold, and a golden waist-chain round her waist, and a pair of golden anklets tinkled above her feet.

If my grandmother were an author how many explanations she would have to offer for this little story! First of all, every one would ask why the king remained twelve years in the forest? Secondly, why should the king's daughter remain unmarried all that while? This would be regarded as absurd.

Even if she could have got so far without a quarrel, still there would have been a great hue and cry about the marriage itself. First, it never happened. Secondly, how could there be a marriage between a princess of the Warrior Caste and a boy of the priestly Brahman Caste? Her readers would have imagined at once that the writer was preaching against our social customs in an underhand way. And they would write letters to the papers.

So I pray with all my heart that my grandmother may be born a grandmother again, and not through some cursed fate take birth as her luckless grandson.

So with a throb of joy and delight, I asked Grannie: "What then?"

Grannie went on: Then the princess took her little husband away in great distress, and built a large palace with seven wings, and began to cherish her husband with great care.

I jumped up and down in my bed and clutched at the bolster more tightly than ever and said: "What then?"

Grannie continued: The little boy went to school and learnt many lessons from his teachers, and as he grew up his class-fellows began to ask him: "Who is that beautiful lady who lives with you in the palace with the seven wings?" The Brahman's son was eager to know who she was. He could only remember how one day he had been gathering sticks, and a great disturbance arose. But all that was so long ago, that he had no clear recollection.

Four or five years passed in this way. His companions always asked him: "Who is that beautiful lady in the palace with the seven wings?" And the Brahman's son would come back from school and sadly tell the princess: "My school companions always ask me who is that beautiful lady in the palace with the seven wings, and I can give them no reply. Tell me, oh, tell me, who you are!"

The princess said: "Let it pass to-day. I will tell you some other day." And every day the Brahman's son would ask; "Who are you?" and the princess would reply: "Let it pass to-day. I will tell you some other day." In this manner four or five more years passed away.

At last the Brahman's son became very impatient, and said: "If you do not tell me to-day who you are, O beautiful lady, I will leave this palace with the seven wings." Then the princess said: "I will certainly tell you to-morrow."

Next day the Brahman's son, as soon as he came home from school, said: "Now, tell me who you are." The princess said: "To-night I will tell you after supper, when you are in bed."

The Brahman's son said: "Very well "; and he began to count the hours in expectation of the night. And the princess, on her side, spread white flowers over the golden bed, and lighted a gold lamp with fragrant oil, and adorned her hair, and dressed herself in a beautiful robe of blue, and began to count the hours in expectation of the night.

That evening when her husband, the Brahman's son, had finished his meal, too excited almost to eat, and had gone to the golden bed in the bed-chamber strewn with flowers, he said to himself: "To-night I shall surely know who this beautiful lady is in the palace with the seven wings."

The princess took for her the food that was left over by her husband, and slowly entered the bed-chamber. She had to answer that night the question, which was the beautiful lady who lived in the palace with the seven wings. And as she went up to the bed to tell him she found a serpent had crept out of the flowers and had bitten the Brahman's son. Her boy-husband was lying on the bed of flowers, with face pale in death.

My heart suddenly ceased to throb, and I asked with choking voice: "What then?"

Grannie said; "Then..."

But what is the use of going on any further with the story? It would only lead on to what was more and more impossible. The boy of seven did not know that, if there were some "What then?" after death, no grandmother of a grandmother could tell us all about it.

But the child's faith never admits defeat, and it would snatch at the mantle of death itself to turn him back. It would be outrageous for him to think that such a story of one teacherless evening could so suddenly come to a stop. Therefore the grandmother had to call back her story from the ever-shut chamber of the great End, but she does it so simply: it is merely by floating the dead body on a banana stem on the river, and having some incantations read by a magician. But in that rainy night and in the dim light of a lamp death loses all its horror in the mind of the boy, and seems nothing more than a deep slumber of a single night. When the story ends the tired eyelids are weighed down with sleep. Thus it is that we send the little body of the child floating on the back of sleep over the still water of time, and then in the morning read a few verses of incantation to restore him to the world of life and light.

4
THE HOME-COMING

Phatik Chakravorti was ringleader among the boys of the village. A new mischief got into his head. There was a heavy log lying on the mud-flat of the river waiting to be shaped into a mast for a boat. He decided that they should all work together to shift the log by main force from its place and roll it away. The owner of the log would be angry and surprised, and they would all enjoy the fun. Every one seconded the proposal, and it was carried unanimously.

But just as the fun was about to begin, Makhan, Phatik's younger brother, sauntered up, and sat down on the log in front of them all without a word. The boys were puzzled for a moment. He was pushed, rather timidly, by one of the boys and told to get up but he remained quite unconcerned. He appeared like a young philosopher meditating on the futility of games. Phatik was furious. "Makhan," he cried, "if you don't get down this minute I'll thrash you!"

Makhan only moved to a more comfortable position.

Now, if Phatik was to keep his regal dignity before the public, it was clear he ought to carry out his threat. But his courage failed him at the crisis. His fertile brain, however, rapidly seized upon a new manoeuvre which would discomfit his brother and afford his followers an added amusement. He gave the word of command to roll the log and Makhan over together. Makhan heard the order, and made it a point of honour to stick on. But he overlooked the fact, like those who attempt earthly fame in other matters, that there was peril in it.

The boys began to heave at the log with all their might, calling out, "One, two, three, go," At the word "go" the log went; and with it went Makhan's philosophy, glory and all.

All the other boys shouted themselves hoarse with delight. But Phatik was a little frightened. He knew what was coming. And, sure enough, Makhan rose from Mother Earth blind as Fate and screaming like the Furies. He rushed at Phatik and scratched his face and beat him and kicked him, and then went crying home. The first act of the drama was over.

Phatik wiped his face, and sat down on the edge of a sunken barge on the river bank, and began to chew a piece of grass. A boat came up to the landing, and a middle-aged man, with grey hair and dark moustache, stepped on shore. He saw the boy sitting there doing nothing, and asked him where the Chakravortis lived. Phatik went on chewing the grass, and said: "Over there," but it was quite impossible to tell where he pointed. The stranger asked him again. He swung his legs to and fro on the side of the barge, and said; "Go and find out," and continued to chew the grass as before.

But now a servant came down from the house, and told Phatik his mother wanted him. Phatik refused to move. But the servant was the master on this occasion. He took Phatik up roughly, and carried him, kicking and struggling in impotent rage.

When Phatik came into the house, his mother saw him. She called out angrily: "So you have been hitting Makhan again?"

Phatik answered indignantly: "No, I haven't; who told you that?"

His mother shouted: "Don't tell lies! You have."

Phatik said suddenly: "I tell you, I haven't. You ask Makhan!" But Makhan thought it best to stick to his previous statement. He said: "Yes, mother. Phatik did hit me."

Phatik's patience was already exhausted. He could not hear this injustice. He rushed at Makhan, and hammered him with blows: "Take that" he cried, "and that, and that, for telling lies."

His mother took Makhan's side in a moment, and pulled Phatik away, beating him with her hands. When Phatik pushed her aside, she shouted out: "What I you little villain! would you hit your own mother?"

It was just at this critical juncture that the grey-haired stranger arrived. He asked what was the matter. Phatik looked sheepish and ashamed.

But when his mother stepped back and looked at the stranger, her anger was changed to surprise. For she recognised her brother, and cried: "Why, Dada! Where have you come from?" As she said these words, she bowed to the ground and touched his feet. Her brother had gone away soon after she had married, and he had started business in Bombay. His sister had lost her husband while he was In Bombay. Bishamber had now come back to Calcutta, and had at once made enquiries about his sister. He had then hastened to see her as soon as he found out where she was.

The next few days were full of rejoicing. The brother asked after the education of the two boys. He was told by his sister that Phatik was a perpetual nuisance. He was lazy, disobedient, and wild. But Makhan was as good as gold, as quiet as a lamb, and very fond of reading, Bishamber kindly offered to take Phatik off his sister's hands, and educate him with his own children in Calcutta. The widowed mother readily agreed. When his uncle asked Phatik If he would like to go to Calcutta with him, his joy knew no bounds, and he said; "Oh, yes, uncle!" In a way that made it quite clear that he meant it.

It was an immense relief to the mother to get rid of Phatik. She had a prejudice against the boy, and no love was lost between the two brothers. She was in daily fear that he would either drown Makhan some day in the river, or break his head in a fight, or run him into some danger or other. At the same time she was somewhat distressed to see Phatik's extreme eagerness to get away.

Phatik, as soon as all was settled, kept asking his uncle every minute when they were to start. He was on pins and needles all day long with excitement, and lay awake most of the night. He bequeathed to Makhan, in perpetuity, his fishing-rod, his big kite and his marbles. Indeed, at this time of departure his generosity towards Makhan was unbounded.

When they reached Calcutta, Phatik made the acquaintance of his aunt for the first time. She was by no means pleased with this unnecessary addition to her family. She found her own three boys quite enough to manage without taking any one else. And to bring a village lad of fourteen into their midst was terribly upsetting. Bishamber should really have thought twice before committing such an indiscretion.

In this world of human affairs there is no worse nuisance than a boy at the age of fourteen. He is neither ornamental, nor useful. It is impossible to shower affection on him as on a little boy; and he is always getting in the way. If he talks with a childish lisp he is called a baby, and if he answers in a grown-up way he is called impertinent. In fact any talk at all from him is resented. Then he is at the unattractive, growing age. He grows out of his clothes with indecent haste; his voice grows hoarse and breaks and quavers; his face grows suddenly angular and unsightly. It is easy to excuse the shortcomings of early childhood, but it is hard to tolerate even unavoidable lapses in a boy of fourteen. The lad himself becomes painfully self-conscious. When he talks with elderly people he is either unduly forward, or else so unduly shy that he appears ashamed of his very existence.

Yet it is at this very age when in his heart of hearts a young lad most craves for recognition and love; and he becomes the devoted slave of any one who shows him consideration. But none dare openly love him, for that would be regarded as undue indulgence, and therefore bad for the boy. So, what with scolding and chiding, he becomes very much like a stray dog that has lost his master.

For a boy of fourteen his own home is the only Paradise. To live in a strange house with strange people is little short of torture, while the height of bliss is to receive the kind looks of women, and never to be slighted by them.

It was anguish to Phatik to be the unwelcome guest in his aunt's house, despised by this elderly woman, and slighted, on every occasion. If she ever asked him to do anything for her, he would be so overjoyed that he would overdo it; and then she would tell him not to be so stupid, but to get on with his lessons.

The cramped atmosphere of neglect in his aunt's house oppressed Phatik so much that he felt that he could hardly breathe. He wanted to go out into the open country and fill his lungs and breathe freely. But there was no open country to go to. Surrounded on all sides by Calcutta houses and walls, he would dream night after night of his village home, and long to be back there. He remembered the glorious meadow where he used to fly his kite all day long; the broad river-banks where he would wander about the livelong day singing and shouting for joy; the narrow brook where he could go and dive and swim at any time he liked. He thought of his band of boy companions over whom he was despot; and, above all, the memory of that tyrant mother of his, who had such a prejudice against him, occupied him day and night. A kind of physical love like that of animals; a longing to be in the presence of the one who is loved; an inexpressible wistfulness during absence; a silent cry of the inmost heart for the mother, like the lowing of a calf in the twilight;-this love, which was almost an animal instinct, agitated the shy, nervous, lean, uncouth and ugly boy. No one could understand it, but it preyed upon his mind continually.

There was no more backward boy in the whole school than Phatik. He gaped and remained silent when the teacher asked him a question, and like an overladen ass patiently suffered all the blows that came down on his back. When other boys were out at play, he stood wistfully by the window and gazed at the roofs of the distant houses. And if by chance he espied children playing on the open terrace of any roof, his heart would ache with longing.

One day he summoned up all his courage, and asked his uncle: "Uncle, when can I go home?"

His uncle answered; "Wait till the holidays come." But the holidays would not come till November, and there was a long time still to wait.

One day Phatik lost his lesson-book. Even with the help of books he had found it very difficult indeed to prepare his lesson. Now it was impossible. Day after day the teacher would cane him unmercifully. His condition became so abjectly miserable that even his cousins were ashamed to own him. They began to jeer and insult him more than the other boys. He went to his aunt at last, and told her that he had lost his book.

His aunt pursed her lips in contempt, and said: "You great clumsy, country lout. How can I afford, with all my family, to buy you new books five times a month?"

That night, on his way back from school, Phatik had a bad headache with a fit of shivering. He felt he was going to have an attack of malarial fever. His one great fear was that he would be a nuisance to his aunt.

The next morning Phatik was nowhere to be seen. All searches in the neighbourhood proved futile. The rain had been pouring in torrents all night, and those who went out in search of the boy got drenched through to the skin. At last Bisbamber asked help from the police.

At the end of the day a police van stopped at the door before the house. It was still raining and the streets were all flooded. Two constables brought out Phatik in their arms and placed him before Bishamber. He was wet through from head to foot, muddy all over, his face and eyes flushed red with fever, and his limbs all trembling. Bishamber carried him in his arms, and took him into the inner apartments. When his wife saw him, she exclaimed; "What a heap of trouble this boy has given us. Hadn't you better send him home?"

Phatik heard her words, and sobbed out loud: "Uncle, I was just going home; but they dragged me back again."

The fever rose very high, and all that night the boy was delirious. Bishamber brought in a doctor. Phatik opened his eyes flushed with fever, and looked up to the ceiling, and said vacantly: "Uncle, have the holidays come yet? May I go home?"

Bishamber wiped the tears from his own eyes, and took Phatik's lean and burning hands in his own, and sat by him through the night. The boy began again to mutter. At last his voice became excited: "Mother," he cried, "don't beat me like that! Mother! I am telling the truth!"

The next day Phatik became conscious for a short time. He turned his eyes about the room, as if expecting some one to come. At last, with an air of disappointment, his head sank back on the pillow. He turned his face to the wall with a deep sigh.

Bishamber knew his thoughts, and, bending down his head, whispered: "Phatik, I have sent for your mother." The day went by. The doctor said in a troubled voice that the boy's condition was very critical.

Phatik began to cry out; "By the mark!--three fathoms. By the mark--four fathoms. By the mark-." He had heard the sailor on the river-steamer calling out the mark on the plumb-line. Now he was himself plumbing an unfathomable sea.

Later in the day Phatik's mother burst into the room like a whirlwind, and began to toss from side to side and moan and cry in a loud voice.

Bishamber tried to calm her agitation, but she flung herself on the bed, and cried: "Phatik, my darling, my darling."

Phatik stopped his restless movements for a moment. His hands ceased beating up and down. He said: "Eh?"

The mother cried again: "Phatik, my darling, my darling."

Phatik very slowly turned his head and, without seeing anybody, said: "Mother, the holidays have come."

5
MY LORD, THE BABY

I

Raicharan was twelve years old when he came as a servant to his master's house. He belonged to the same caste as his master, and was given his master's little son to nurse. As time went on the boy left Raicharan's arms to go to school. From school he went on to college, and after college he entered the judicial service. Always, until he married, Raicharan was his sole attendant.

But, when a mistress came into the house, Raicharan found two masters instead of one. All his former influence passed to the new mistress. This was compensated for by a fresh arrival. Anukul had a son born to him, and Raicharan by his unsparing attentions soon got a complete hold over the child. He used to toss him up in his arms, call to him in absurd baby language, put his face close to the baby's and draw it away again with a grin.

Presently the child was able to crawl and cross the doorway. When Raicharan went to catch him, he would scream with mischievous laughter and make for safety. Raicharan was amazed at the profound skill and exact judgment the baby showed when pursued. He would say to his mistress with a look of awe and mystery: "Your son will be a judge some day."

New wonders came in their turn. When the baby began to toddle, that was to Raicharan an epoch in human history. When he called his father Ba-ba and his mother Ma-ma and Raicharan Chan-na, then Raicharan's ecstasy knew no bounds. He went out to tell the news to all the world.

After a while Raicharan was asked to show his ingenuity in other ways. He had, for instance, to play the part of a horse, holding the reins between his teeth and prancing with his feet. He had also to wrestle with his little charge, and if he could not, by a wrestler's trick, fall on his back defeated at the end, a great outcry was certain.

About this time Anukul was transferred to a district on the banks of the Padma. On his way through Calcutta he bought his son a little go-cart. He bought him also a yellow satin waistcoat, a gold-laced cap, and some gold bracelets and anklets. Raicharan was wont to take these out, and put them on his little charge with ceremonial pride, whenever they went for a walk.

Then came the rainy season, and day after day the rain poured down in torrents. The hungry river, like an enormous serpent, swallowed down terraces, villages, cornfields, and covered with its flood the tall grasses and wild casuarinas on the sand-banks. From time to time there was a deep thud, as the river-banks crumbled. The unceasing roar of the rain current could be beard from far away. Masses of foam, carried swiftly past, proved to the eye the swiftness of the stream.

One afternoon the rain cleared. It was cloudy, but cool and bright. Raicharan's little despot did not want to stay in on such a fine afternoon. His lordship climbed into the go-cart. Raicharan, between the shafts, dragged him slowly along till he reached the rice-fields on the banks of the river. There was no one in the fields, and no boat on the stream. Across the water, on the farther side, the clouds were rifted in the west. The silent ceremonial of the setting sun was revealed in all its glowing splendour. In the midst of that stillness the child, all of a sudden, pointed with his finger in front of him and cried: "Chan-nal Pitty fow."

Close by on a mud-flat stood a large Kadamba tree in full flower. My lord, the baby, looked at it with greedy eyes, and Raicharan knew his meaning. Only a short time before he had made, out of these very flower balls, a small go-cart; and the child had been so entirely happy dragging it about with a string, that for the whole day Raicharan was not made to put on the reins at all. He was promoted from a horse into a groom.

But Raicharan had no wish that evening to go splashing knee-deep through the mud to reach the flowers. So he quickly pointed his finger in the opposite direction, calling out: "Oh, look, baby, look! Look at the bird." And with all sorts of curious noises he pushed the go-cart rapidly away from the tree.

But a child, destined to be a judge, cannot be put off so easily. And besides, there was at the time nothing to attract his eyes. And you cannot keep up for ever the pretence of an imaginary bird.

The little Master's mind was made up, and Raicharan was at his wits' end. "Very well, baby," he said at last, "you sit still in the cart, and I'll go and get you the pretty flower. Only mind you don't go near the water."

As he said this, he made his legs bare to the knee, and waded through the oozing mud towards the tree.

The moment Raicharan had gone, his little Master went off at racing speed to the forbidden water. The baby saw the river rushing by, splashing and gurgling as it went. It seemed as though the disobedient wavelets themselves were running away from some greater Raicharan with the laughter of a thousand children. At the sight of their mischief, the heart of the human child grew excited and restless. He got down stealthily from the go-cart and toddled off towards the river. On his way he picked up a small stick, and leant over the bank of the stream pretending to fish. The mischievous fairies of the river with their mysterious voices seemed inviting him into their play-house.

Raicharan had plucked a handful of flowers from the tree, and was carrying them back in the end of his cloth, with his face wreathed in smiles. But when he reached the go-cart, there was no one there. He looked on all sides and there was no one there. He looked back at the cart and there was no one there.

In that first terrible moment his blood froze within him. Before his eyes the whole universe swam round like a dark mist. From the depth of his broken heart he gave one piercing cry; "Master, Master, little Master."

But no voice answered "Chan-na." No child laughed mischievously back; no scream of baby delight welcomed his return. Only the river ran on, with its splashing, gurgling noise as before,--as though it knew nothing at all, and had no time to attend to such a tiny human event as the death of a child.

As the evening passed by Raicharan's mistress became very anxious. She sent men out on all sides to search. They went with lanterns in their hands, and reached at last the banks of the Padma. There they found Raicharan rushing up and down the fields, like a stormy wind, shouting the cry of despair: "Master, Master, little Master!"

When they got Raicharan home at last, he fell prostrate at his mistress's feet. They shook him, and questioned him, and asked him repeatedly where he had left the child; but all he could say was, that he knew nothing.

Though every one held the opinion that the Padma had swallowed the child, there was a lurking doubt left in the mind. For a band of gipsies had been noticed outside the village that afternoon, and some suspicion rested on them. The mother went so far in her wild grief as to think it possible that Raicharan himself had stolen the child. She called him aside with piteous entreaty and said: "Raicharan, give me back my baby. Oh! give me back my child. Take from me any money you ask, but give me back my child!"

Raicharan only beat his forehead in reply. His mistress ordered him out of the house.

Artukul tried to reason his wife out of this wholly unjust suspicion: "Why on earth," he said, "should he commit such a crime as that?"

The mother only replied: "The baby had gold ornaments on his body. Who knows?"

It was impossible to reason with her after that.

II

Raicharan went back to his own village. Up to this time he had had no son, and there was no hope that any child would now be born to him. But it came about before the end of a year that his wife gave birth to a son and died.

All overwhelming resentment at first grew up in Raicharan's heart at the sight of this new baby. At the back of his mind was resentful suspicion that it had come as a usurper in place of the little Master. He also thought it would be a grave offence to be happy with a son of his own after what had happened to his master's little child. Indeed, if it had not been for a widowed sister, who mothered the new baby, it would not have lived long.

But a change gradually came over Raicharan's mind. A wonderful thing happened. This new baby in turn began to crawl about, and cross the doorway with mischief in its face. It also showed an amusing cleverness in making its escape to safety. Its voice, its sounds of laughter and tears, its gestures, were those of the little Master. On some days, when Raicharan listened to its crying, his heart suddenly began thumping wildly against his ribs, and it seemed to him that his former little Master was crying somewhere in the unknown land of death because he had lost his Chan-na.

Phailna (for that was the name Raicharan's sister gave to the new baby) soon began to talk. It learnt to say Ba-ba and Ma-ma with a baby accent. When Raicharan heard those familiar sounds the mystery suddenly became clear. The little Master could not cast off the spell of his Chan-na, and therefore he had been reborn in his own house.

The arguments in favour of this were, to Raicharan, altogether beyond dispute:

1. The new baby was born soon after his little master's death.
2. His wife could never have accumulated such merit as to give birth to a son in middle age.
3. The new baby walked with a toddle and called out Ba-ba and Ma-ma. There was no sign lacking which marked out the future judge.

Then suddenly Raicharan remembered that terrible accusation of the mother. "Ah," he said to himself with amazement, "the mother's heart was right. She knew I had stolen her child." When once he had come to this conclusion, he was filled with remorse for his past neglect. He now gave himself over, body and soul, to the new baby, and became its devoted attendant. He began to bring it up, as if it were the son of a rich man. He bought a go-cart, a yellow satin waistcoat, and a gold-embroidered cap. He melted down the ornaments of his dead wife, and made gold bangles and anklets. He refused to let the little child play with any one of the neighbourhood, and became himself its sole companion day and night. As the baby grew up to boyhood, he was so petted and spoilt and clad in such finery that the village children would call him "Your Lordship," and jeer at him; and older people regarded Raicharan as unaccountably crazy about the child.

At last the time came for the boy to go to school. Raicharan sold his small piece of land, and went to Calcutta. There he got employment with great difficulty as a servant, and sent Phailna to school. He spared no pains to give him the best education, the best clothes, the best food. Meanwhile he lived himself on a mere handful of rice, and would say in secret: "Ah! my little Master, my dear little Master, you loved me so much that you came back to my house. You shall never suffer from any neglect of mine."

Twelve years passed away in this manner. The boy was able to read and write well. He was bright and healthy and good-looking. He paid a great deal of attention to his personal appearance, and was specially careful in parting his hair. He was inclined to extravagance and finery, and spent money freely. He could never quite look on Raicharan as a father, because, though fatherly in affection, he had the manner of a servant. A further fault was this, that Raicharan kept secret from every one that himself was the father of the child.

The students of the hostel, where Phailna was a boarder, were greatly amused by Raicharan's country manners, and I have to confess that behind his father's back Phailna joined in their fun. But, in the bottom of their hearts, all the students loved the innocent and tender-hearted old man, and Phailna was very fond of him also. But, as I have said before, he loved him with a kind of condescension.

Raicharan grew older and older, and his employer was continually finding fault with him for his incompetent work. He had been starving himself for the boy's sake. So he had grown physically weak, and no longer up to his work. He would forget things, and his mind became dull and stupid. But his employer expected a full servant's work out of him, and would not brook excuses. The money that Raicharan had brought with him from the sale of his land was exhausted. The boy was continually grumbling about his clothes, and asking for more money.

Raicharan made up his mind. He gave up the situation where he was working as a servant, and left some money with Phailna and said: "I have some business to do at home in my village, and shall be back soon."

He went off at once to Baraset where Anukul was magistrate. Anukul's wife was still broken down with grief. She had had no other child.

One day Anukul was resting after a long and weary day in court. His wife was buying, at an exorbitant price, a herb from a mendicant quack, which was said to ensure the birth of a child. A voice of greeting was heard in the courtyard. Anukul went out to see who was there. It was Raicharan. Anukul's heart was softened when he saw his old servant. He asked him many questions, and offered to take him back into service.

Raicharan smiled faintly, and said in reply; "I want to make obeisance to my mistress."

Anukul went with Raicharan into the house, where the mistress did not receive him as warmly as his old master. Raicharan took no notice of this, but folded his hands, and said: "It was not the Padma that stole your baby. It was I."

Anukul exclaimed: "Great God! Eh! What! Where is he?" Raicharan replied: "He is with me, I will bring him the day after to-morrow."

It was Sunday. There was no magistrate's court sitting. Both husband and wife were looking expectantly along the road, waiting from early morning for Raicharan's appearance. At ten o'clock he came, leading Phailna by the hand.

Anukul's wife, without a question, took the boy into her lap, and was wild with excitement, sometimes laughing, sometimes weeping, touching him, kissing his hair and his forehead, and gazing into his face with hungry, eager eyes. The boy was very good-looking and dressed like a gentleman's son. The heart of Anukul brimmed over with a sudden rush of affection.

Nevertheless the magistrate in him asked: "Have you any proofs?" Raicharan said: "How could there be any proof of such a deed? God alone knows that I stole your boy, and no one else in the world."

When Anukul saw how eagerly his wife was clinging to the boy, he realised the futility of asking for proofs. It would be wiser to believe. And then--where could an old man like Raicharan get such a boy from? And why should his faithful servant deceive him for nothing?

"But," he added severely, "Raicharan, you must not stay here."

"Where shall I go, Master?" said Raicharan, in a choking voice, folding his hands; "I am old. Who will take in an old man as a servant?"

The mistress said: "Let him stay. My child will be pleased. I forgive him."

But Anukul's magisterial conscience would not allow him. "No," he said, "he cannot be forgiven for what he has done."

Raicharan bowed to the ground, and clasped Anukul's feet. "Master," he cried, "let me stay. It was not I who did it. It was God."

Anukul's conscience was worse stricken than ever, when Raicharan tried to put the blame on God's shoulders.

"No," he said, "I could not allow it. I cannot trust you any more. You have done an act of treachery."

Raicharan rose to his feet and said: "It was not I who did it."

"Who was it then?" asked Anukul.

Raicharan replied: "It was my fate."

But no educated man could take this for an excuse. Anukul remained obdurate.

When Phailna saw that he was the wealthy magistrate's son, and not Raicharan's, he was angry at first, thinking that he had been cheated all this time of his birthright. But seeing Raicharan in distress, he generously said to his father: "Father, forgive him. Even if you don't let him live with us, let him have a small monthly pension."

After hearing this, Raicharan did not utter another word. He looked for the last time on the face of his son; he made obeisance to his old master and mistress. Then he went out, and was mingled with the numberless people of the world.

At the end of the month Anukul sent him some money to his village. But the money came back. There was no one there of the name of Raicharan.

6
THE KINGDOM OF CARDS

I

Once upon a time there was a lonely island in a distant sea where lived the Kings and Queens, the Aces and the Knaves, in the Kingdom of Cards. The Tens and Nines, with the Twos and Threes, and all the other members, had long ago settled there also. But these were not twice-born people, like the famous Court Cards.

The Ace, the King, and the Knave were the three highest castes. The fourth Caste was made up of a mixture of the lower Cards. The Twos and Threes were lowest of all. These inferior Cards were never allowed to sit in the same row with the great Court Cards.

Wonderful indeed were the regulations and rules of that island kingdom. The particular rank of each individual had been settled from time immemorial. Every one had his own appointed work, and never did anything else. An unseen hand appeared to be directing them wherever they went,--according to the Rules.

No one in the Kingdom of Cards had any occasion to think: no one had any need to come to any decision: no one was ever required to debate any new subject. The citizens all moved along in a listless groove without speech. When they fell, they made no noise. They lay down on their backs, and gazed upward at the sky with each prim feature firmly fixed for ever.

There was a remarkable stillness in the Kingdom of Cards. Satisfaction and contentment were complete in all their rounded wholeness. There was never any uproar or violence. There was never any excitement or enthusiasm.

The great ocean, crooning its lullaby with one unceasing melody, lapped the island to sleep with a thousand soft touches of its wave's white hands. The vast sky, like the outspread azure wings of the brooding mother-bird, nestled the island round with its downy plume. For on the distant horizon a deep blue line betokened another shore. But no sound of quarrel or strife could reach the Island of Cards, to break its calm repose.

II

In that far-off foreign land across the sea, there lived a young Prince whose mother was a sorrowing queen. This queen had fallen from favour, and was living with her only son on the seashore. The Prince passed his childhood alone and forlorn, sitting by his forlorn mother, weaving the net of his big desires. He longed to go in search of the Flying Horse, the Jewel in the Cobra's hood, the Rose of Heaven, the Magic Roads, or to find where the Princess Beauty was sleeping in the Ogre's castle over the thirteen rivers and across the seven seas.

From the Son of the Merchant at school the young Prince learnt the stories of foreign kingdoms. From the Son of the Kotwal he learnt the adventures of the Two Genii of the Lamp. And when the rain came beating down, and the clouds covered the sky, he would sit on the threshold facing the sea, and say to his sorrowing mother: "Tell me, mother, a story of some very far-off land."

And his mother would tell him an endless tale she had heard in her childhood of a wonderful country beyond the sea where dwelt the Princess Beauty. And the heart of the young Prince would become sick with longing, as he sat on the threshold, looking out on the ocean, listening to his mother's wonderful story, while the rain outside came beating down and the grey clouds covered the sky.

One day the Son of the Merchant came to the Prince, and said boldly: "Comrade, my studies are over. I am now setting out on my travels to seek my fortunes on the sea. I have come to bid you good-bye."

The Prince said; "I will go with you."

And the Son of Kotwal said also: "Comrades, trusty and true, you will not leave me behind. I also will be your companion."

Then the young Prince said to his sorrowing mother; "Mother, I am now setting out on my travels to seek my fortune. When I come back once more, I shall surely have found some way to remove all your sorrow."

So the Three Companions set out on their travels together. In the harbour were anchored the twelve ships of the merchant, and the Three Companions got on board. The south wind was blowing, and the twelve ships sailed away, as fast as the desires which rose in the Prince's breast.

At the Conch Shell Island they filled one ship with conchs. At the Sandal Wood Island they filled a second ship with sandal-wood, and at the Coral Island they filled a third ship with coral.

Four years passed away, and they filled four more ships, one with ivory, one with musk, one with cloves, and one with nutmegs.

But when these ships were all loaded a terrible tempest arose. The ships were all of them sunk, with their cloves and nutmeg, and musk and ivory, and coral and sandal-wood and conchs. But the ship with the Three Companions struck on an island reef, buried them safe ashore, and itself broke in pieces.

This was the famous Island of Cards, where lived the Ace and King and Queen and Knave, with the Nines and Tens and all the other Members--according to the Rules.

III

Up till now there had been nothing to disturb that island stillness. No new thing had ever happened. No discussion had ever been held.

And then, of a sudden, the Three Companions appeared, thrown up by the sea,--and the Great Debate began. There were three main points of dispute.

First, to what caste should these unclassed strangers belong? Should they rank with the Court Cards? Or were they merely lower-caste people, to be ranked with the Nines and Tens? No precedent could be quoted to decide this weighty question.

Secondly, what was their clan? Had they the fairer hue and bright complexion of the Hearts, or was theirs the darker complexion of the Clubs? Over this question there were interminable disputes. The whole marriage system of the island, with its intricate regulations, would depend on its nice adjustment.

Thirdly, what food should they take? With whom should they live and sleep? And should their heads be placed south-west, north-west, or only north-east? In all the Kingdom of Cards a series of problems so vital and critical had never been debated before.

But the Three Companions grew desperately hungry. They had to get food in some way or other. So while this debate went on, with its interminable silence and pauses, and while the Aces called their own meeting, and formed themselves into a Committee, to find some obsolete dealing with the question, the Three Companions themselves were eating all they could find, and drinking out of every vessel, and breaking all regulations.

Even the Twos and Threes were shocked at this outrageous behaviour. The Threes said; "Brother Twos, these people are openly shameless!" And the Twos said: "Brother Threes, they are evidently of lower caste than ourselves!" After their meal was over, the Three Companions went for a stroll in the city.

When they saw the ponderous people moving in their dismal processions with prim and solemn faces, then the Prince turned to the Son of the Merchant and the Son of the Kotwal, and threw back his head, and gave one stupendous laugh.

Down Royal Street and across Ace Square and along the Knave Embankment ran the quiver of this strange, unheard-of laughter, the laughter that, amazed at itself, expired in the vast vacuum of silence.

The Son of the Kotwal and the Son of the Merchant were chilled through to the bone by the ghost-like stillness around them. They turned to the Prince, and said: "Comrade, let us away. Let us not stop for a moment in this awful land of ghosts."

But the Prince said: "Comrades, these people resemble men, so I am going to find out, by shaking them upside down and outside in, whether they have a single drop of warm living blood left in their veins."

IV

The days passed one by one, and the placid existence of the Island went on almost without a ripple. The Three Companions obeyed no rules nor regulations. They never did anything correctly either in sitting or standing or turning themselves round or lying on their back. On the contrary, wherever they saw these things going on precisely and exactly according to the Rules, they gave way to inordinate laughter. They remained unimpressed altogether by the eternal gravity of those eternal regulations.

One day the great Court Cards came to the Son of the Kotwal and the Son of the Merchant and the Prince.

"Why," they asked slowly, "are you not moving according to the Rules?"

The Three Companions answered: "Because that is our Ichcha (wish)."

The great Court Cards with hollow, cavernous voices, as if slowly awakening from an age-long dream, said together: "Ich-cha! And pray who is Ich-cha?"

They could not understand who Ichcha was then, but the whole island was to understand it by-and-by. The first glimmer of light passed the threshold of their minds when they found out, through watching the actions of the Prince, that they might move in a straight line in an opposite direction from the one in which they had always gone before. Then they made another startling discovery, that there was another side to the Cards which they had never yet noticed with attention. This was the beginning of the change.

Now that the change had begun, the Three Companions were able to initiate them more and more deeply into the mysteries of Ichcha. The Cards gradually became aware that life was not bound by regulations. They began to feel a secret satisfaction in the kingly power of choosing for themselves.

But with this first impact of Ichcha the whole pack of cards began to totter slowly, and then tumble down to the ground. The scene was like that of some huge python awaking from a long sleep, as it slowly unfolds its numberless coils with a quiver that runs through its whole frame.

V

Hitherto the Queens of Spades and Clubs and Diamonds and Hearts had remained behind curtains with eyes that gazed vacantly into space, or else remained fixed upon the ground.

And now, all of a sudden, on an afternoon in spring the Queen of Hearts from the balcony raised her dark eyebrows for a moment, and cast a single glance upon the Prince from the corner of her eye.

"Great God," cried the Prince, "I thought they were all painted images. But I am wrong. They are women after all."

Then the young Prince called to his side his two Companions, and said in a meditative voice; "My comrades! There is a charm about these ladies that I never noticed before. When I saw that glance of the Queen's dark, luminous eyes, brightening with new emotion, it seemed to me like the first faint streak of dawn in a newly created world."

The two Companions smiled a knowing smile, and said: "Is that really so, Prince?"

And the poor Queen of Hearts from that day went from bad to worse. She began to forget all rules in a truly scandalous manner. If, for instance, her place in the row was beside the Knave, she suddenly found herself quite accidentally standing beside the Prince instead. At this, the Knave, with motionless face and solemn voice, would say: "Queen, you have made a mistake."

And the poor Queen of Hearts' red cheeks would get redder than ever. But the Prince would come gallantly to her rescue and say: "No! There is no mistake. From to-day I am going to be Knave!"

Now it came to pass that, while every one was trying to correct the improprieties of the guilty Queen of Hearts, they began to make mistakes themselves. The Aces found themselves elbowed out by the Kings. The Kings got muddled up with the Knaves. The Nines and Tens assumed airs as though they belonged to the Great Court Cards. The Twos and Threes were found secretly taking the places specially resented for the Fours and Fives. Confusion had never been so confounded before.

Many spring seasons had come and gone in that Island of Cards. The Kokil, the bird of Spring, had sung its song year after year. But it had never stirred the blood as it stirred it now. In days gone by the sea had sung its tireless melody. But, then, it had proclaimed only the inflexible monotony of the Rule. And suddenly its waves were telling, through all their flashing light and luminous shade and myriad voices, the deepest yearnings of the heart of love!

VI

Where are vanished now their prim, round, regular, complacent features? Here is a face full of love-sick longing. Here is a heart heating wild with regrets. Here is a mind racked sore with doubts. Music and sighing, and smiles and tears, are filling the air. Life is throbbing; hearts are breaking; passions are kindling.

Every one is now thinking of his own appearance, and comparing himself with others. The Ace of Clubs is musing to himself, that the King of Spades may be just passably good-looking. "But," says he, "when I walk down the street you have only to see how people's eyes turn towards me." The King of Spades is saying; "Why on earth is that Ace of Clubs always straining his neck and strutting about like a peacock? He imagines all the Queens are dying of love for him, while the real fact is--" Here he pauses, and examines his face in the glass.

But the Queens were the worst of all. They began to spend all their time in dressing themselves up to the Nines. And the Nines would become their hopeless and abject slaves. But their cutting remarks about one another were more shocking still.

So the young men would sit listless on the leaves under the trees, lolling with outstretched limbs in the forest shade. And the young maidens, dressed in pale-blue robes, would come walking accidentally to the same shade of the same forest by the same trees, and turn their eyes as though they saw no one there, and look as though they came out to see nothing at all. And then one young man more forward than the rest in a fit of madness would dare to go near to a maiden in blue. But, as he drew near, speech would forsake him. He would stand there tongue-tied and foolish, and the favourable moment would pass.

The Kokil birds were singing in the boughs overhead. The mischievous South wind was blowing; it disarrayed the hair, it whispered in the ear, and stirred the music in the blood. The leaves of the trees were murmuring with rustling delight. And the ceaseless sound of the ocean made all the mute longings of the heart of man and maid surge backwards and forwards on the full springtide of love.

The Three Companions had brought into the dried-up channels of the Kingdom of Cards the full flood-tide of a new life.

VII

And, though the tide was full, there-was a pause as though the rising waters would not break into foam but remain suspended for ever. There were no outspoken words, only a cautious going forward one step and receding two. All seemed busy heaping up their unfulfilled desires like castles in the air, or fortresses of sand. They were pale and speechless, their eyes were burning, their lips trembling with unspoken secrets.

The Prince saw what was wrong. He summoned every one on the Island and said: "Bring hither the flutes and the cymbals, the pipes and drums. Let all be played together, and raise loud shouts of rejoicing. For the Queen of Hearts this very night is going to choose her Mate!"

So the Tens and Nines began to blow on their flutes and pipes; the Eights and Sevens played on their sackbuts and viols; and even the Twos and Threes began to beat madly on their drums.

When this tumultous gust of music came, it swept away at one blast all those sighings and mopings. And then what a torrent of laughter and words poured forth! There were daring proposals and locking refusals, and gossip and chatter, and jests and merriment. It was like the swaying and shaking, and rustling and soughing, in a summer gale, of a million leaves and branches in the depth of the primeval forest.

But the Queen of Hearts, in a rose-red robe, sat silent in the shadow of her secret bower, and listened to the great uproarious sound of music and mirth, that came floating towards her. She shut her eyes, and dreamt her dream of lore. And when she opened them she found the Prince seated on the ground before her gazing up at her face. And she covered her eyes with both hands, and shrank back quivering with an inward tumult of joy.

And the Prince passed the whole day alone, walking by the side of the surging sea. He carried in his mind that startled look, that shrinking gesture of the Queen, and his heart beat high with hope.

That night the serried, gaily-dressed ranks of young men and maidens waited with smiling faces at the Palace Gates. The Palace Hall was lighted with fairy lamps and festooned with the flowers of spring. Slowly the Queen of Hearts entered, and the whole assembly rose to greet her. With a jasmine garland in her hand, she stood before the

Prince with downcast eyes. In her lowly bashfulness she could hardly raise the garland to the neck of the Mate she had chosen. But the Prince bowed his head, and the garland slipped to its place. The assembly of youths and maidens had waited her choice with eager, expectant hush. And when the choice was made, the whole vast concourse rocked and swayed with a tumult of wild delight. And the sound of their shouts was heard in every part of the island, and by ships far out at sea. Never had such a shout been raised in the Kingdom of Cards before.

And they carried the Prince and his Bride, and seated them on the throne, and crowned them then and there in the Ancient Island of Cards.

And the sorrowing Mother Queen, on the 'far-off island shore on the other side of the sea, came sailing to her son's new kingdom in a ship adorned with gold.

And the citizens are no longer regulated according to the Rules, but are good or bad, or both, according to their Ichcha.

7
THE DEVOTEE

At a time, when my unpopularity with a part of my readers had reached the nadir of its glory, and my name had become the central orb of the journals, to be attended through space with a perpetual rotation of revilement, I felt the necessity to retire to some quiet place and endeavour to forget my own existence.

I have a house in the country some miles away from Calcutta, where I can remain unknown and unmolested. The villagers there have not, as yet, come to any conclusion about me. They know I am no mere holiday-maker or pleasure-seeker; for I never outrage the silence of the village nights with the riotous noises of the city. Nor do they regard me as ascetic, because the little acquaintance they have of me carries the savour of comfort about it. I am not, to them, a traveller; for, though I am a vagabond by nature, my wandering through the village fields is aimless. They are hardly even quite certain whether I am married or single; for they have never seen me with my children. So, not being able to classify me in any animal or vegetable kingdom that they know, they have long since given me up and left me stolidly alone.

But quite lately I have come to know that there is one person in the village who is deeply interested in me. Our acquaintance began on a sultry afternoon in July. There had been rain all the morning, and the air was still wet and heavy with mist, like eyelids when weeping is over.

I sat lazily watching a dappled cow grazing on the high bank of the river. The afternoon sun was playing on her glossy hide. The simple beauty of this dress of light made me wonder idly at man's deliberate waste of money in setting up tailors' shops to deprive his own skin of its natural clothing.

While I was thus watching and lazily musing, a woman of middle age came and prostrated herself before me, touching the ground with her forehead. She carried in her robe some bunches of flowers, one of which she offered to me with folded hands. She said to me, as she offered it: "This is an offering to my God."

She went away. I was so taken aback as she uttered these words, that I could hardly catch a glimpse of her before she was gone. The whole incident was entirely simple, but it left a deep impression on my mind; and as I turned back once more to look at the cattle in the field, the zest of life in the cow, who was munching the lush grass with deep breaths, while she whisked off the flies, appeared to me fraught with mystery. My readers may laugh at my foolishness, but my heart was full of adoration. I offered my worship to the pure joy of living, which is God's own life. Then, plucking a tender shoot from the mango tree, I fed the cow with it from my own hand, and as I did this I had the satisfaction of having pleased my God.

The next year when I returned to the village it was February. The cold season still lingered on. The morning sun came into my room, and I was grateful for its warmth. I was writing, when the servant came to tell me that a devotee, of the Vishnu cult, wanted to see me. I told him, in an absent way, to bring her upstairs, and went on with my writing. The Devotee came in, and bowed to me, touching my feet. I found that she was the same woman whom I had met, for a brief moment, a year ago.

I was able now to examine her more closely. She was past that age when one asks the question whether a woman is beautiful or not. Her stature was above the ordinary height, and she was strongly built; but her body was slightly bent owing to her constant attitude of veneration. Her manner had nothing shrinking about it. The most remarkable of her features were her two eyes. They seemed to have a penetrating power which could make distance near.

With those two large eyes of hers, she seemed to push me as she entered.

"What is this?" she asked. "Why have you brought me here before your throne, my God? I used to see you among the trees; and that was much better. That was the true place to meet you."

She must have seen me walking in the garden without my seeing her. For the last few clays, however, I had suffered from a cold, and had been prevented from going out. I had, perforce, to stay indoors and pay my homage to the evening sky from my terrace. After a silent pause the Devotee said to me: "O my God, give me some words of good."

I was quite unprepared for this abrupt request, and answered her on the spur of the moment: "Good words I neither give nor receive. I simply open my eyes and keep silence, and then I can at once both hear and see, even when no sound is uttered. Now, while I am looking at you, it is as good as listening to your voice."

The Devotee became quite excited as I spoke, and exclaimed: "God speaks to me, not only with His mouth, but with His whole body."

I said to her: "When I am silent I can listen with my whole body. I have come away from Calcutta here to listen to that sound."

The Devotee said: "Yes, I know that, and therefore I have come here to sit by you."

Before taking her leave, she again bowed to me, and touched my feet. I could see that she was distressed, because my feet were covered. She wished them to be bare.

Early next morning I came out, and sat on my terrace on the roof. Beyond the line of trees southward I could see the open country chill and desolate. I could watch the sun rising over the sugar-cane in the East, beyond the clump of trees at the side of the village. Out of the deep shadow of those dark trees the village road suddenly appeared. It stretched forward, winding its way to some distant villages on the horizon, till it was lost in the grey of the mist.

That morning it was difficult to say whether the sun had risen or not. A white fog was still clinging to the tops of the trees. I saw the Devotee walking through the blurred dawn, like a mist-wraith of the morning twilight. She was singing her chant to God, and sounding her cymbals.

The thick haze lifted at last; and the sun, like the kindly grandsire of the village, took his seat amid all the work that was going on in home and field.

When I had just settled down at my writing-table, to appease the hungry appetite of my editor in Calcutta, there came a sound of footsteps on the stair, and the Devotee, humming a tune to herself, entered, and bowed before me. I lifted my head from my papers.

She said to me: "My God, yesterday I took as sacred food what was left over from your meal."

I was startled, and asked her how she could do that.

"Oh," she said, "I waited at your door in the evening, while you were at dinner, and took some food from your plate when it was carried out."

This was a surprise to me, for every one in the village knew that I had been to Europe, and had eaten with Europeans. I was a vegetarian, no doubt, but the sanctity of my cook would not bear investigation, and the orthodox regarded my food as polluted.

The Devotee, noticing my sign of surprise, said: "My God, why should I come to you at all, if I could not take your food?"

I asked her what her own caste people would say. She told me she had already spread the news far and wide all over the village. The caste people had shaken their heads, but agreed that she must go her own way.

I found out that the Devotee came from a good family in the country, and that her mother was well to-do, and desired to keep her daughter. But she preferred to be a mendicant. I asked her how she made her living. She told me that her followers had given her a piece of land, and that she begged her food from door to door. She said to me: "The food which I get by begging is divine."

After I had thought over what she said, I understood her meaning. When we get our food precariously as alms, we remember God the giver. But when we receive our food regularly at home, as a matter of course, we are apt to regard it as ours by right.

I had a great desire to ask her about her husband. But as she never mentioned him even indirectly, I did not question her.

I found out very soon that the Devotee had no respect at all for that part of the village where the people of the higher castes lived.

"They never give," she said, "a single farthing to God's service; and yet they have the largest share of God's glebe. But the poor worship and starve."

I asked her why she did not go and live among these godless people, and help them towards a better life. "That," I said with some unction, "would be the highest form of divine worship."

I had heard sermons of this kind from time to time, and I am rather fond of copying them myself for the public benefit, when the chance comes.

But the Devotee was not at all impressed. She raised her big round eyes, and looked straight into mine, and said:

"You mean to say that because God is with the sinners, therefore when you do them any service you do it to God? Is that so?"

"Yes," I replied, "that is my meaning."

"Of course," she answered almost impatiently, "of course, God is with them: otherwise, how could they go on living at all? But what is that to me? My God is not there. My God cannot be worshipped among them; because I do not find Him there. I seek Him where I can find Him."

As she spoke, she made obeisance to me. What she meant to say was really this. A mere doctrine of God's omnipresence does not help us. That God is all-pervading,--this truth may be a mere intangible abstraction, and therefore unreal to ourselves. Where I can see Him, there is His reality in my soul.

I need not explain that all the while she showered her devotion on me she did it to me not as an individual. I was simply a vehicle of her divine worship. It was not for me either to receive it or to refuse it: for it was not mine, but God's.

When the Devotee came again, she found me once more engaged with my books and papers.

"What have you been doing," she said, with evident vexation, "that my God should make you undertake such drudgery? Whenever I come, I find you reading and writing."

"God keeps his useless people busy," I answered; "otherwise they would be bound to get into mischief. They have to do all the least necessary things in life. It keeps them out of trouble."

The Devotee told me that she could not bear the encumbrances, with which, day by day, I was surrounded. If she wanted to see me, she was not allowed by the servants to come straight upstairs. If she wanted to touch my feet in worship, there were my socks always in the way. And when she wanted to have a simple talk with me, she found my mind lost in a wilderness of letters.

This time, before she left me, she folded her hands, and said: "My God! I felt your feet in my breast this morning. Oh, how cool! And they were bare, not covered. I held them upon my head for a long time in worship. That filled my very being. Then, after that, pray what was the use of my coming to you yourself? Why did I come? My Lord, tell me truly,--wasn't it a mere infatuation?"

There were some flowers in my vase on the table. While she was there, the gardener brought some new flowers to put in their place. The Devotee saw him changing them.

"Is that all?" she exclaimed. "Have you done with the flowers? Then give them to me."

She held the flowers tenderly in the cup of her hands, and began to gaze at them with bent head. After a few moments' silence she raised her head again, and said to me: "You never look at these flowers; therefore they become stale to you. If you would only look into them, then your reading and writing would go to the winds."

She tied the flowers together in the end of her robe, and placed them, in an attitude of worship, on the top of her head, saying reverently: "Let me carry my God with me."

While she did this, I felt that flowers in our rooms do not receive their due meed of loving care at our hands. When we stick them in vases, they are more like a row of naughty schoolboys standing on a form to be punished.

The Devotee came again the same evening, and sat by my feet on the terrace of the roof.

"I gave away those flowers," she said, "as I went from house to house this morning, singing God's name. Beni, the head man of our village, laughed at me for my devotion, and said: 'Why do you waste all this devotion on Him? Don't you know He is reviled up and down the countryside?' Is that true, my God? Is it true that they are hard upon you?"

For a moment I shrank into myself. It was a shock to find that the stains of printers' ink could reach so far.

The Devotee went on: "Beni imagined that he could blow out the flame of my devotion at one breath! But this is no mere tiny flame: it is a burning fire. Why do they abuse you, my God?"

I said: "Because I deserved it. I suppose in my greed I was loitering about to steal people's hearts in secret."

The Devotee said: "Now you see for yourself how little their hearts are worth. They are full of poison, and this will cure you of your greed."

"When a man," I answered, "has greed in his heart, he is always on the verge of being beaten. The greed itself supplies his enemies with poison."

"Our merciful God," she replied, "beats us with His own hand, and drives away all the poison. He who endures God's beating to the end is saved."

II

That evening the Devotee told me the story of her life. The stars of evening rose and set behind the trees, as she went on to the end of her tale.

"My husband is very simple. Some people think that he is a simpleton; but I know that those who understand simply, understand truly. In business and household management he was able to hold his own. Because his needs were small, and his wants few, he could manage carefully on what we had. He would never meddle in other matters, nor try to understand them.

"Both my husband's parents died before we had been married long, and we were left alone. But my husband always needed some one to be over him. I am ashamed to confess that he had a sort of reverence for me, and looked upon me as his superior. But I am sure that he could understand things better than I, though I had greater powers of talking.

"Of all the people in the world he held his Guru Thakur (spiritual master) in the highest veneration. Indeed it was not veneration merely but love; and such love as his is rare.

"Guru Thakur was younger than my husband. Oh! how beautiful he was!

"My husband had played games with him when he was a boy; and from that time forward he had dedicated his heart and soul to this friend of his early days. Thakur knew how simple my husband was, and used to tease him mercilessly.

"He and his comrades would play jokes upon him for their own amusement; but he would bear them all with longsuffering.

"When I married into this family, Guru Thakur was studying at Benares. My husband used to pay all his expenses. I was eighteen years old when he returned home to our village.

"At the age of fifteen I had my child. I was so young I did not know how to take care of him. I was fond of gossip, and liked to be with my village friends for hours together. I used to get quite cross with my boy when I was compelled to stay at home and nurse him. Alas! my child-God came into my life, but His playthings were not ready for Him. He came to the mother's heart, but the mother's heart lagged behind. He left me in anger; and ever since I have been searching for Him up and down the world.

"The boy was the joy of his father's life. My careless neglect used to pain my husband. But his was a mute soul. He has never been able to give expression to his pain.

"The wonderful thing was this, that in spite of my neglect the child used to love me more than any one else. He seemed to have the dread that I would one day go away and leave him. So even when I was with him, he would watch me with a restless look in his eyes. He had me very little to himself, and therefore his desire to be with me was always painfully eager. When I went each day to the river, he used to fret and stretch out his little arms to be taken with me. But the bathing ghal was my place for meeting my friends, and I did not care to burden myself with the child.

"It was an early morning in August. Fold after fold of grey clouds had wrapped the mid-day round with a wet clinging robe. I asked the maid to take care of the boy, while I went down to the river. The child cried after me as I went away.

"There was no one there at the bathing ghat when I arrived. As a swimmer, I was the best among all the village women. The river was quite full with the rains. I swam out into the middle of the stream some distance from the shore.

"Then I heard a cry from the bank, 'Mother!' I turned my head and saw my boy coming down the steps, calling me as he came. I shouted to him to stop, but he went on, laughing and calling. My feet and hands became cramped with fear. I shut my eyes, afraid to see. When I opened them, there, at the slippery stairs, my boy's ripple of laughter had disappeared for ever.

"I got back to the shore. I raised him from the water. I took him in my arms, my boy, my darling, who had begged so often in vain for me to take him. I took him now, but he no more looked in my eyes and called 'Mother.'

"My child-God had come. I had ever neglected Him. I had ever made Him cry. And now all that neglect began to beat against my own heart, blow upon blow, blow upon blow. When my boy was with me, I had left him alone. I had refused to take him with me. And now, when he is dead, his memory clings to me and never leaves me.

"God alone knows all that my husband suffered. If he had only punished me for my sin, it would have been better for us both. But he knew only how to endure in silence, not how to speak.

"When I was almost mad with grief, Guru Thakur came back. In earlier days, the relation between him and my husband had been that of boyish friendship. Now, my husband's reverence for his sanctity and learning was unbounded. He could hardly speak in his presence, his awe of him was so great.

"My husband asked his Guru to try to give me some consolation. Guru Thakur began to read and explain to me the scriptures. But I do not think they had much effect on my mind. All their value for me lay in the voice that uttered them. God makes the draught of divine life deepest in the heart for man to drink, through the human voice. He has no better vessel in His hand than that; and He Himself drinks His divine draught out of the same vessel.

"My husband's love and veneration for his Guru filled our house, as incense fills a temple shrine. I showed that veneration, and had peace. I saw my God in the form of that Guru. He used to come to take his meal at our house every morning. The first thought that would come to my mind on waking from sleep was that of his food as a sacred gift from God. When I prepared the things for his meal, my fingers would sing for joy.

"When my husband saw my devotion to his Guru, his respect for me greatly increased. He noticed his Guru's eager desire to explain the scriptures to me. He used to think that he could never expect to earn any regard from his Guru himself, on account of his stupidity; but his wife had made up for it.

"Thus another five years went by happily, and my whole life would have passed like that; but beneath the surface some stealing was going on somewhere in secret. I could not detect it; but it was detected by the God of my heart. Then came a day when, in a moment our whole life was turned upside down.

"It was a morning in midsummer. I was returning home from bathing, my clothes all wet, down a shady lane. At the bend of the road, under the mango tree, I met my Guru Thakur. He had his towel on his shoulder and was repeating some Sanskrit verses as he was going to take his bath. With my wet clothes clinging all about me I was ashamed to meet him. I tried to pass by quickly, and avoid being seen. He called me by my name.

"I stopped, lowering my eyes, shrinking into myself. He fixed his gaze upon me, and said: 'How beautiful is your body!'

"All the universe of birds seemed to break into song in the branches overhead. All the bushes in the lane seemed ablaze with flowers. It was as though the earth and sky and everything had become a riot of intoxicating joy.

"I cannot tell how I got home. I only remember that I rushed into the room where we worship God. But the room seemed empty. Only before my eyes those same gold spangles of light were dancing which had quivered in front of me in that shady lane on my way back from the river.

"Guru Thakur came to take his food that day, and asked my husband where I had gone. He searched for me, but could not find me anywhere.

"Ah! I have not the same earth now any longer. The same sunlight is not mine. I called on my God in my dismay, and He kept His face turned away from me.

"The day passed, I know not how. That night I had to meet my husband. But the night is dark and silent. It is the time when my husband's mind comes out shining, like stars at twilight. I had heard him speak things in the dark, and I had been surprised to find how deeply he understood.

"Sometimes I am late in the evening in going to rest on account of household work. My husband waits for me, seated on the floor, without going to bed. Our talk at such times had often begun with something about our Guru.

"That night, when it was past midnight, I came to my room, and found my husband sleeping on the floor. Without disturbing him I lay down on the ground at his feet, my head towards him. Once he stretched his feet, while sleeping, and struck me on the breast. That was his last bequest.

"Next morning, when my husband woke up from his sleep, I was already sitting by him. Outside the window, over the thick foliage of the jack-fruit tree, appeared the first pale red of the dawn at the fringe of the night. It was so early that the crows had not yet begun to call.

"I bowed, and touched my husband's feet with my forehead. He sat up, starting as if waking from a dream, and looked at my face in amazement. I said:

"'I have made up my mind. I must leave the world. I cannot belong to you any longer. I must leave your home.'

"Perhaps my husband thought that he was still dreaming. He said not a word.

"'Ah! do hear me!' I pleaded with infinite pain. 'Do hear me and understand! You must marry another wife. I must take my leave.'

"My husband said: 'What is all this wild, mad talk? Who advises you to leave the world?'

"I said: 'My Guru Thakur.'

"My husband looked bewildered. 'Guru Thakur!' he cried. 'When did he give you this advice?'

"'In the morning,' I answered, 'yesterday, when I met him on my way back from the river.'

"His voice trembled a little. He turned, and looked in my face, and asked me: 'Why did he give you such a behest?'

"'I do not know,' I answered. 'Ask him! He will tell you himself, if he can.'

"My husband said: 'It is possible to leave the world, even when continuing to live in it. You need not leave my home. I will speak to my Guru about it.'

"'Your Guru,' I said, 'may accept your petition; but my heart will never give its consent. I must leave your home. From henceforth, the world is no more to me.'

"My husband remained silent, and we sat there on the floor in the dark. When it was light, he said to me: 'Let us both come to him.'

"I folded my hands and said: 'I shall never meet him again.'

"He looked into my face. I lowered my eyes. He said no more. I knew that, somehow, he had seen into my mind, and understood what was there. In this world of mine, there were only two who loved me best--my boy and my husband. That love was my God, and therefore it could brook no falsehood. One of these two left me, and I left the other. Now I must have truth, and truth alone."

She touched the ground at my feet, rose and bowed to me, and departed.

8
VISION

I

When I was a very young wife, I gave birth to a dead child, and came near to death myself. I recovered strength very slowly, and my eyesight became weaker and weaker.

My husband at this time was studying medicine. He was not altogether sorry to have a chance of testing his medical knowledge on me. So he began to treat my eyes himself.

My elder brother was reading for his law examination. One day he came to see me, and was alarmed at my condition.

"What are you doing?" he said to my husband. "You are ruining Kumo's eyes. You ought to consult a good doctor at once."

My husband said irritably: "Why! what can a good doctor do more than I am doing? The case is quite a simple one, and the remedies are all well known."

Dada answered with scorn: "I suppose you think there is no difference between you and a Professor in your own Medical College."

My husband replied angrily: "If you ever get married, and there is a dispute about your wife's property, you won't take my advice about Law. Why, then, do you now come advising me about Medicine?"

While they were quarrelling, I was saying to myself that it was always the poor grass that suffered most when two kings went to war. Here was a dispute going on between these two, and I had to bear the brunt of it.

It also seemed to me very unfair that, when my family had given me in marriage, they should interfere afterwards. After all, my pleasure and pain are my husband's concern, not theirs.

From that day forward, merely over this trifling matter of my eyes, the bond between my husband and Dada was strained.

To my surprise one afternoon, while my husband was away, Dada brought a doctor in to see me. He examined my eyes very carefully, and looked grave. He said that further neglect would be dangerous. He wrote out a prescription, and Dada for the medicine at once. When the strange doctor had gone, I implored my Dada not to interfere. I was sure that only evil would come from the stealthy visits of a doctor.

I was surprised at myself for plucking up courage speak to my brother like that. I had always hitherto been afraid of him. I am sure also that Dada was surprised at my boldness. He kept silence for a while, and then said to me: "Very well, Kumo. I won't call in the doctor any more. But when the medicine comes you must take it."

Dada then went away. The medicine came from chemist. I took it--bottles, powders, prescriptions and all--and threw it down the well!

My husband had been irritated by Dada's interference, and he began to treat my eyes with greater diligence than ever. He tried all sorts of remedies. I bandaged my eyes as he told me, I wore his coloured glasses, I put in his drops, I took all his powders. I even drank the cod-liver oil he gave me, though my gorge rose against it.

Each time he came back from the hospital, he would ask me anxiously how I felt; and I would answer: "Oh! much better." Indeed I became an expert in self-delusion. When I found that the water in my eyes was still increasing, I would console myself with the thought that it was a good thing to get rid of so much bad fluid; and, when the flow of water in my eyes decreased, I was elated at my husband's skill.

But after a while the agony became unbearable. My eyesight faded away, and I had continual headaches day and night. I saw how much alarmed my husband was getting. I gathered from his manner that he was casting about for a pretext to call in a doctor. So I hinted that it might be as well to call one in.

That he was greatly relieved, I could see. He called in an English doctor that very day. I do not know what talk they had together, but I gathered that the Sahib had spoken very sharply to my husband.

He remained silent for some time after the doctor had gone. I took his hands in mine, and said: "What an ill-mannered brute that was! Why didn't you call in an Indian doctor? That would have been much better. Do you think that man knows better than you do about my eyes?"

My husband was very silent for a moment, and then said with a broken voice: "Kumo, your eyes must be operated on."

I pretended to be vexed with him for concealing the fact from me so long.

"Here you have known this all the time," said I, "and yet you have said nothing about it! Do you think I am such a baby as to be afraid of an operation?"

At that he regained his good spirits: "There are very few men," said he, "who are heroic enough to look forward to an operation without shrinking."

I laughed at him: "Yes, that is so. Men are heroic only before their wives!"

He looked at me gravely, and said: "You are perfectly right. We men are dreadfully vain."

I laughed away his seriousness: "Are you sure you can beat us women even in vanity?"

When Dada came, I took him aside: "Dada, that treatment your doctor recommended would have done me a world of good; only unfortunately. I mistook the mixture for the lotion. And since the day I made the mistake, my eyes have grown steadily worse; and now an operation is needed."

Dada said to me: "You were under your husband's treatment, and that is why I gave up coming to visit you."

"No," I answered. "In reality, I was secretly treating myself in accordance with your doctor's directions."

Oh! what lies we women have to tell! When we are mothers, we tell lies to pacify our children; and when we are wives, we tell lies to pacify the fathers of our children. We are never free from this necessity.

My deception had the effect of bringing about a better feeling between my husband and Dada. Dada blamed himself for asking me to keep a secret from my husband: and my husband regretted that he had not taken my brother's advice at the first.

At last, with the consent of both, an English doctor came, and operated on my left eye. That eye, however, was too weak to bear the strain; and the last flickering glimmer of light went out. Then the other eye gradually lost itself in darkness.

One day my husband came to my bedside. "I cannot brazen it out before you any longer," said he, "Kumo, it is I who have ruined your eyes."

I felt that his voice was choking with tears, and so I took up his right hand in both of mine and said: "Why! you did exactly what was right. You have dealt only with that which was your very own. Just imagine, if some strange doctor had come and taken away my eyesight. What consolation should I have had then? But now I can feel that all has happened for the best; and my great comfort is to know that it is at your hands I have lost my eyes. When Ramchandra found one lotus too few with which to worship God, he offered both his eyes in place of the lotus. And I hate dedicated my eyes to my God. From now, whenever you see something that is a joy to you, then you must describe it to me; and I will feed upon your words as a sacred gift left over from your vision."

I do not mean, of course, that I said all this there and then, for it is impossible to speak these things an the spur of the moment. But I used to think over words like these for days and days together. And when I was very depressed, or if at any time the light of my devotion became dim, and I pitied my evil fate, then I made my mind utter these sentences, one by one, as a child repeats a story that is told. And so I could breathe once more the serener air of peace and love.

At the very time of our talk together, I said enough to show my husband what was in my heart.

"Kumo," he said to me, "the mischief I have done by my folly can never be made good. But I can do one thing. I can ever remain by your side, and try to make up for your want of vision as much as is in my power."

"No," said I. "That will never do. I shall not ask you to turn your house into an hospital for the blind. There is only one thing to be done, you must marry again."

As I tried to explain to him that this was necessary, my voice broke a little. I coughed, and tried to hide my emotion, but he burst out saying:

"Kumo, I know I am a fool, and a braggart, and all that, but I am not a villain! If ever I marry again, I swear to you--I swear to you the most solemn oath by my family god, Gopinath--may that most hated of all sins, the sin of parricide, fall on my head!"

Ah! I should never, never have allowed him to swear that dreadful oath. But tears were choking my voice, and I could not say a word for insufferable joy. I hid my blind face in my pillows, and sobbed, and sobbed again. At last, when the first flood of my tears was over, I drew his head down to my breast.

"Ah!" said I, "why did you take such a terrible oath? Do you think I asked you to marry again for your own sordid pleasure? No! I was thinking of myself, for she could perform those services which were mine to give you when I had my sight."

"Services!" said he, "services! Those can be done by servants. Do you think I am mad enough to bring a slave into my house, and bid her share the throne with this my Goddess?"

As he said the word "Goddess," he held up my face in his hands, and placed a kiss between my brows. At that moment the third eye of divine wisdom was opened, where he kissed me, and verily I had a consecration.

I said in my own mind: "It is well. I am no longer able to serve him in the lower world of household cares. But I shall rise to a higher region. I shall bring down blessings from above. No more lies! No more deceptions for me! All the littlenesses and hypocrisies of my former life shall be banished for ever!"

That day, the whole day through, I felt a conflict going on within me. The joy of the thought, that after this solemn oath it was impossible for my husband to marry again, fixed its roots deep in my heart, and I could not tear them out. But the new Goddess, who had taken her new throne in me, said: "The time might come when it would be good for your husband to break his oath and marry again." But the woman, who was within me, said: "That may be; but all the same an oath is an oath, and there is no way out." The Goddess, who was within me, answered: "That is no reason why you should exult over it." But the woman, who was within me, replied: "What you say is quite true, no doubt; all the same he has taken his oath." And the same story went on again and again. At last the Goddess frowned in silence, and the darkness of a horrible fear came down upon me.

My repentant husband would not let the servants do my work; he must do it all himself. At first it gave me unbounded delight to be dependent on him thus for every little thing. It was a means of keeping him by my side, and my desire to have him with me had become intense since my blindness. That share of his presence, which my eyes had lost, my other senses craved. When he was absent from my side, I would feel as if I were hanging in mid-air, and had lost my hold of all things tangible.

Formerly, when my husband came back late from the hospital, I used to open my window and gaze at the road. That road was the link which connected his world with mine. Now when I had lost that link through my blindness, all my body would go out to seek him. The bridge that united us had given way, and there was now this unsurpassable chasm. When he left my side the gulf seemed to yawn wide open. I could only wait for the time when he should cross back again from his own shore to mine.

But such intense longing and such utter dependence can never be good. A wife is a burden enough to a man, in all conscience, and to add to it the burden of this blindness was to make his life unbearable. I vowed that I would suffer alone, and never wrap my husband round in the folds of my all-pervading darkness.

Within an incredibly short space of time I managed to train myself to do all my household duties by the help of touch and sound and smell. In fact I soon found that I could get on with greater skill than before. For sight often distracts rather than helps us. And so it came to pass that, when these roving eyes of mine could do their work no longer, all the other senses took up their several duties with quietude and completeness.

When I had gained experience by constant practice, I would not let my husband do any more household duties for me. He complained bitterly at first that I was depriving him of his penance.

This did not convince me. Whatever he might say, I could feel that he had a real sense of relief when these household duties were over. To serve daily a wife who is blind can never make up the life of a man.

II

My husband at last had finished his medical course. He went away from Calcutta to a small town to practise as a doctor. There in the country I felt with joy, through all my blindness, that I was restored to the arms of my mother. I had left my village birthplace for Calcutta when I was eight years old. Since then ten years had passed away, and in the great city the memory of my village home had grown dim. As long as I had eyesight, Calcutta with its busy life screened from view the memory of my early days. But when I lost my eyesight I knew for the first time that Calcutta allured only the eyes: it could not fill the mind. And now, in my blindness, the scenes of my childhood shone out once more, like stars that appear one by one in the evening sky at the end of the day.

It was the beginning of November when we left Calcutta for Harsingpur. The place was new to me, but the scents and sounds of the countryside pressed round and embraced me. The morning breeze coming fresh from the newly ploughed land, the sweet and tender smell of the flowering mustard, the shepherd-boy's flute sounding in the distance, even the creaking noise of the bullock-cart, as it groaned over the broken village road, filled my world with delight. The memory of my past life, with all its ineffable fragrance and sound, became a living present to me, and my blind eyes could not tell me I was wrong. I went back, and lived over again my childhood. Only one thing was absent: my mother was not with me.

I could see my home with the large peepul trees growing along the edge of the village pool. I could picture in my mind's eye my old grandmother seated on the ground with her thin wisps of hair untied, warming her back in the sun as she made the little round lentil balls to be dried and used for cooking. But somehow I could not recall the songs she used to croon to herself in her weak and quavering voice. In the evening, whenever I heard the lowing of cattle, I could almost watch the figure of my mother going round the sheds with lighted lamp in her hand. The smell of the wet fodder and the pungent smoke of the straw fire would enter into my very heart. And in the distance I seemed to hear the clanging of the temple bell wafted up by the breeze from the river bank.

Calcutta, with all its turmoil and gossip, curdles the heart. There, all the beautiful duties of life lose their freshness and innocence. I remember one day, when a friend of mine came in, and said to me: "Kumo, why don't you feel angry? If I had been treated like you by my husband, I would never look upon his face again."

She tried to make me indignant, because he had been so long calling in a doctor.

"My blindness," said I, "was itself a sufficient evil. Why should I make it worse by allowing hatred to grow up against my husband?"

My friend shook her head in great contempt, when she heard such old-fashioned talk from the lips of a mere chit of a girl. She went away in disdain. But whatever might be my answer at the time, such words as these left their poison; and the venom was never wholly got out of the soul, when once they had been uttered.

So you see Calcutta, with its never-ending gossip, does harden the heart. But when I came back to the country all my earlier hopes and faiths, all that I held true in life during childhood, became fresh and bright once more. God came to me, and filled my heart and my world. I bowed to Him, and said:

"It is well that Thou has taken away my eyes. Thou art with me."

Ah! But I said more than was right. It was a presumption to say: "Thou art with me." All we can say is this: "I must be true to Thee." Even when nothing is left for us, still we have to go on living.

III

We passed a few happy months together. My husband gained some reputation in his profession as a doctor. And money came with it.

But there is a mischief in money. I cannot point to any one event; but, because the blind have keener perceptions than other people, I could discern the change which came over my husband along with the increase of wealth.

He had a keen sense of justice when he was younger, and had often told me of his great desire to help the poor when once he obtained a practice of his own. He had a noble contempt far those in his profession who would not feel the pulse of a poor patient before collecting his fee. But now I noticed a difference. He had become strangely hard. Once when a poor woman came, and begged him, out of charity, to save the life of her only child, he bluntly refused. And when I implored him myself to help her, he did his work perfunctorily.

While we were less rich my husband disliked sharp practice in money matters. He was scrupulously honourable in such things. But since he had got a large account at the bank he was often closeted for hours with some scamp of a landlord's agent, for purposes which clearly boded no good.

Where has he drifted? What has become of this husband of mine,-- the husband I knew before I was blind; the husband who kissed me that day between my brows, and enshrined me on the throne of a Goddess? Those whom a sudden gust of passion brings down to the dust can rise up again with a new strong impulse of goodness. But those who, day by day, become dried up in the very fibre of their moral being; those who by some outer parasitic growth choke the inner life by slow degrees,-- such wench one day a deadness which knows no healing.

The separation caused by blindness is the merest physical trifle. But, ah! it suffocates me to find that he is no longer with me, where he stood with me in that hour when we both knew that I was blind. That is a separation indeed!

I, with my love fresh and my faith unbroken, have kept to the shelter of my heart's inner shrine. But my husband has left the cool shade of those things that are ageless and unfading. He is fast disappearing into the barren, waterless waste in his mad thirst for gold.

Sometimes the suspicion comes to me that things not so bad as they seem: that perhaps I exaggerate because I am blind. It may be that, if my eyesight were unimpaired, I should have accepted world as I found it. This, at any rate, was the light in which my husband looked at all my moods and fancies.

One day an old Musalman came to the house. He asked my husband to visit his little grand-daughter. I could hear the old man say: "Baba, I am a poor man; but come with me, and Allah will do you good." My husband answered coldly: "What Allah will do won't help matters; I want to know what you can do for me."

When I heard it, I wondered in my mind why God had not made me deaf as well as blind. The old man heaved a deep sigh, and departed. I sent my maid to fetch him to my room. I met him at the door of the inner apartment, and put some money into his hand.

"Please take this from me," said I, "for your little grand-daughter, and get a trustworthy doctor to look after her. And-pray for my husband."

But the whole of that day I could take no food at all. In the afternoon, when my husband got up from sleep, he asked me: "Why do you look so pale?"

I was about to say, as I used to do in the past: "Oh! It's nothing "; but those days of deception were over, and I spoke to him plainly.

"I have been hesitating," I said, "for days together to tell you something. It has been hard to think out what exactly it was I wanted to say. Even now I may not be able to explain what I had in my mind. But I am sure you know what has happened. Our lives have drifted apart."

My husband laughed in a forced manner, and said: "Change is the law of nature."

I said to him: "I know that. But there are some things that are eternal."

Then he became serious.

"There are many women," said he, "who have a real cause for sorrow. There are some whose husbands do not earn money. There are others whose husbands do not love them. But you are making yourself wretched about nothing at all."

Then it became clear to me that my very blindness had conferred on me the power of seeing a world which is beyond all change. Yes! It is true. I am not like other women. And my husband will never understand me.

IV

Our two lives went on with their dull routine for some time. Then there was a break in the monotony. An aunt of my husband came to pay us a visit.

The first thing she blurted out after our first greeting was this: "Well, Krum, it's a great pity you have become blind; but why do you impose your own affliction on your husband? You must get him to another wife."

There was an awkward pause. If my husband had only said something in jest, or laughed in her face, all would have been over. But he stammered and hesitated, and said at last in a nervous, stupid way: "Do you really think so? Really, Aunt, you shouldn't talk like that."

His aunt appealed to me. "Was I wrong, Kumo?"

I laughed a hollow laugh.

"Had not you better," said I, "consult some one more competent to decide? The pickpocket never asks permission from the man whose pocket he is going to pick."

"You are quite right," she replied blandly. "Abinash, my dear, let us have our little conference in private. What do you say to that?"

After a few days my husband asked her, in my presence, if she knew of any girl of a decent family who could come and help me in my household work. He knew quite well that I needed no help. I kept silence.

"Oh! there are heaps of them," replied his aunt. "My cousin has a daughter who is just of the marriageable age, and as nice a girl as you could wish. Her people would be only too glad to secure you as a husband."

Again there came from him that forced, hesitating laugh, and he said: "But I never mentioned marriage."

"How could you expect," asked his aunt, "a girl of decent family to come and live in your house without marriage?"

He had to admit that this was reasonable, and remained nervously silent.

I stood alone within the closed doors of my blindness after he had gone, and called upon my God and prayed: "O God, save my husband."

When I was coming out of the household shrine from my morning worship a few days later, his aunt took hold of both my hands warmly.

"Kumo, here is the girl," said she, "we were speaking about the other day. Her name is Hemangini. She will be delighted to meet you. Hemo, come here and be introduced to your sister."

My husband entered the room at the same moment. He feigned surprise when he saw the strange girl, and was about to retire. But his aunt said: "Abinash, my dear, what are you running away for? There is no need to do that. Here is my cousin's daughter, Hemangini, come to see you. Hemo, make your bow to him."

As if taken quite by surprise, he began to ply his aunt with questions about the when and why and how of the new arrival.

I saw the hollowness of the whole thing, and took Hemangini by the hand and led her to my own room. I gently stroked her face and arms and hair, and found that she was about fifteen years old, and very beautiful.

As I felt her face, she suddenly burst out laughing and said: "Why! what are you doing? Are you hypnotising me?"

That sweet ringing laughter of hers swept away in a moment all the dark clouds that stood between us. I threw my right arm about her neck.

"Dear one," said I, "I am trying to see you." And again I stroked her soft face with my left hand.

"Trying to see me?" she said, with a new burst of laughter. "Am I like a vegetable marrow, grown in your garden, that you want to feel me all round to see how soft I am?"

I suddenly bethought me that she did not know I had lost my sight.

"Sister, I am blind," said I.

She was silent. I could feel her big young eyes, full of curiosity, peering into my face. I knew they were full of pity. Then she grew thoughtful and puzzled, and said, after a short pause:

"Oh! I see now. That was the reason your husband invited his aunt to come and stay here."

"No!" I replied, "you are quite mistaken. He did not ask her to come. She came of her own accord."

Hemangini went off into a peal of laughter. "That's just like my aunt," said she. "Oh I wasn't it nice of her to come without any invitation? But now she's come, you won't get her to move for some time, I can assure you!"

Then she paused, and looked puzzled.

"But why did father send me?" she asked. "Can you tell me that?"

The aunt had come into the room while we were talking. Hemangini said to her: "When are you thinking of going back, Aunt?"

The aunt looked very much upset.

"What a question to ask!" said she, "I've never seen such a restless body as you. We've only just come, and you ask when we're going back!"

"It is all very well for you," Hemangini said, "for this house belongs to your near relations. But what about me? I tell you plainly I can't stop here." And then she held my hand and said: "What do you think, dear?"

I drew her to my heart, but said nothing. The aunt was in a great difficulty. She felt the situation was getting beyond her control; so she proposed that she and her niece should go out together to bathe.

"No! we two will go together," said Hemangini, clinging to me. The aunt gave in, fearing opposition if she tried to drag her away.

Going down to the river Hemangini asked me: "Why don't you have children?"

I was startled by her question, and answered: "How can I tell? My God has not given me any. That is the reason."

"No! That's not the reason," said Hemangini quickly. "You must have committed some sin. Look at my aunt. She is childless. It must be because her heart has some wickedness. But what wickedness is in your heart?"

The words hurt me. I have no solution to offer for the problem of evil. I sighed deeply, and said in the silence of my soul: "My God! Thou knowest the reason."

"Gracious goodness," cried Hemangini, "what are you sighing for? No one ever takes me seriously."

And her laughter pealed across the river.

V

I found out after this that there were constant interruptions in my husband's professional duties. He refused all calls from a distance, and would hurry away from his patients, even when they were close at hand.

Formerly it was only during the mid-day meals and at night-time that he could come into the inner apartment. But now, with unnecessary anxiety for his aunt's comfort, he began to visit her at all hours of the day. I knew at once that he had come to her room, when I heard her shouting for Hemangini to bring in a glass of water. At first the girl would do what she was told; but later on she refused altogether.

Then the aunt would call, in an endearing voice: "Hemo! Hemo! Hemangini." But the girl would cling to me with an impulse of pity. A sense of dread and sadness would keep her silent. Sometimes she would shrink towards me like a hunted thing, who scarcely knew what was coming.

About this time my brother came down from Calcutta to visit me. I knew how keen his powers of observation were, and what a hard judge he was. I feared my husband would be put on his defence, and have to stand his trial before him. So I endeavoured to hide the true situation behind a mask of noisy cheerfulness. But I am afraid I overdid the part: it was unnatural for me.

My husband began to fidget openly, and asked how long my brother was going to stay. At last his impatience became little short of insulting, and my brother had no help for it but to leave. Before going he placed his hand on my head, and kept it there for some time. I noticed that his hand shook, and a tear fell from his eyes, as he silently gave me his blessing.

I well remember that it was an evening in April, and a market-day. People who had come into the town were going back home from market.

There was the feeling of an impending storm in the air; the smell of the wet earth and the moisture in the wind were all-pervading. I never keep a lighted lamp in my bedroom, when I am alone, lest my clothes should catch fire, or some accident happen. I sat on the floor in my dark room, and called upon the God of my blind world.

"O my Lord," I cried, "Thy face is hidden. I cannot see. I am blind. I hold tight this broken rudder of a heart till my hands bleed. The waves have become too strong for me. How long wilt thou try me, my God, how long?"

I kept my head prone upon the bedstead and began to sob. As I did so, I felt the bedstead move a little. The next moment Hemangini was by my side. She clung to my neck, and wiped my tears away silently. I do not know why she had been waiting that evening in the inner room, or why she had been lying alone there in the dusk. She asked me no question. She said no word. She simply placed her cool hand on my forehead, and kissed me, and departed.

The next morning Hemangini said to her aunt in my presence: "If you want to stay on, you can. But I don't. I'm going away home with our family servant."

The aunt said there was no need for her to go alone, for she was going away also. Then smilingly and mincingly she brought out, from a plush case, a ring set with pearls.

"Look, Hemo," said she, "what a beautiful ring my Abinash brought for you."

Hemangini snatched the ring from her hand.

"Look, Aunt," she answered quickly, "just see how splendidly I aim." And she flung the ring into the tank outside the window.

The aunt, overwhelmed with alarm, vexation, and surprise, bristled like a hedgehog. She turned to me, and held me by the hand.

"Kumo," she repeated again and again, "don't say a word about this childish freak to Abinash. He would be fearfully vexed."

I assured her that she need not fear. Not a word would reach him about it from my lips.

The next day before starting for home Hemangini embraced me, and said: "Dearest, keep me in mind; do not forget me."

I stroked her face over and over with my fingers, and said: "Sister, the blind have long memories."

I drew her head towards me, and kissed her hair and her forehead. My world suddenly became grey. All the beauty and laughter and tender youth, which had nestled so close to me, vanished when Hemangini departed. I went groping about with arms outstretched, seeking to find out what was left in my deserted world.

My husband came in later. He affected a great relief now that they were gone, but it was exaggerated and empty. He pretended that his aunt's visit had kept him away from work.

Hitherto there had been only the one barrier of blindness between me and my husband. Now another barrier was added,--this deliberate silence about Hemangini. He feigned utter indifference, but I knew he was having letters about her.

It was early in May. My maid entered my room one morning, and asked me: "What is all this preparation going on at the landing on the river? Where is Master going?"

I knew there was something impending, but I said to the maid: "I can't say."

The maid did not dare to ask me any more questions. She sighed, and went away.

Late that night my husband came to me.

"I have to visit a patient in the country," said he. "I shall have to start very early to-morrow morning, and I may have to be away for two or three days."

I got up from my bed. I stood before him, and cried aloud: "Why are you telling me lies?"

My husband stammered out: "What--what lies have I told you?"

I said: "You are going to get married."

He remained silent. For some moments there was no sound in the room. Then I broke the silence:

"Answer me," I cried. "Say, yes."

He answered, "Yes," like a feeble echo.

I shouted out with a loud voice: "No! I shall never allow you. I shall save you from this great disaster, this dreadful sin. If I fail in this, then why am I your wife, and why did I ever worship my God?"

The room remained still as a stone. I dropped on the floor, and clung to my husband's knees.

"What have I done?" I asked. "Where have I been lacking? Tell me truly. Why do you want another wife?"

My husband said slowly: "I will tell you the truth. I am afraid of you. Your blindness has enclosed you in its fortress, and I have now no entrance. To me you are no longer a woman. You are awful as my God. I cannot live my every day life with you. I want a woman--just an ordinary woman--whom I can be free to chide and coax and pet and scold."

Oh, tear open my heart and see! What am I else but that,--just an ordinary woman? I am the same girl that I was when I was newly wed, a girl with all her need to believe, to confide, to worship.

I do not recollect exactly the words that I uttered. I only remember that I said: "If I be a true wife, then, may God be my witness, you shall never do this wicked deed, you shall never break your oath. Before you commit such sacrilege, either I shall become a widow, or Hemangini shall die."

Then I fell down on the floor in a swoon. When I came to myself, it was still dark. The birds were silent. My husband had gone.

All that day I sat at my worship in the sanctuary at the household shrine. In the evening a fierce storm, with thunder and lightning and rain, swept down upon the house and shook it. As I crouched before the shrine, I did not ask my God to save my husband from the storm, though he must have been at that time in peril on the river. I prayed that whatever might happen to me, my husband might be saved from this great sin.

Night passed. The whole of the next day I kept my seat at worship. When it was evening there was the noise of shaking and beating at the door. When the door was broken open, they found me lying unconscious on the ground, and carried me to my room.

When I came to myself at last, I heard some one whispering in my ear: "Sister."

I found that I was lying in my room with my head on Hemangini's lap. When my head moved, I heard her dress rustle. It was the sound of bridal silk.

O my God, my God! My prayer has gone unheeded! My husband has fallen!

Hemangini bent her head low, and said in a sweet whisper: "Sister, dearest, I have come to ask your blessing on our marriage."

At first my whole body stiffened like the trunk of a tree that has been struck by lightning. Then I sat up, and said, painfully, forcing myself to speak the words: "Why should I not bless you? You have done no wrong."

Hemangini laughed her merry laugh.

"Wrong!" said she. "When you married it was right; and when I marry, you call it wrong!"

I tried to smile in answer to her laughter. I said in my mind: "My prayer is not the final thing in this world. His will is all. Let the blows descend upon my head; but may they leave my faith and hope in God untouched."

Hemangini bowed to me, and touched my feet. "May you be happy," said I, blessing her, "and enjoy unbroken prosperity."

Hemangini was still unsatisfied.

"Dearest sister," she said, "a blessing for me is not enough. You must make our happiness complete. You must, with those saintly hands of yours, accept into your home my husband also. Let me bring him to you."

I said: "Yes, bring him to me."

A few moments later I heard a familiar footstep, and the question, "Kumo, how are you?"

I started up, and bowed to the ground, and cried: "Dada!"

Hemangini burst out laughing.

"You still call him elder brother?" she asked. "What nonsense! Call him younger brother now, and pull his ears and cease him, for he has married me, your younger sister."

Then I understood. My husband had been saved from that great sin. He had not fallen.

I knew my Dada had determined never to marry. And, since my

mother had died, there was no sacred wish of hers to implore him to wedlock. But I, his sister, by my sore need bad brought it to pass. He had married for my sake.

Tears of joy gushed from my eyes, and poured down my cheeks. I tried, but I could not stop them. Dada slowly passed his fingers through my hair. Hemangini clung to me, and went on laughing.

I was lying awake in my bed for the best part of the night, waiting with straining anxiety for my husband's return. I could not imagine how he would bear the shock of shame and disappointment.

When it was long past the hour of midnight, slowly my door opened. I sat up on my bed, and listened. They were the footsteps of my husband. My heart began to beat wildly. He came up to my bed, held my band in his.

"Your Dada," said he, "has saved me from destruction. I was being dragged down and down by a moments madness. An infatuation had seized me, from which I seemed unable to escape. God alone knows what a load I was carrying on that day when I entered the boat. The storm came down on river, and covered the sky. In the midst of all fears I had a secret wish in my heart to be drowned, and so disentangle my life from the knot which I had tied it. I reached Mathurganj. There I heard the news which set me free. Your brother had married Hemangini. I cannot tell you with what joy and shame I heard it. I hastened on board the boat again. In that moment of self-revelation I knew that I could have no happiness except with you. You are a Goddess."

I laughed and cried at the same time, and said: "No, no, no! I am not going to be a Goddess any longer I am simply your own little wife. I am an ordinary woman."

"Dearest," he replied, "I have also something I want to say to you. Never again put me to shame by calling me your God."

On the next day the little town became joyous with sound of conch shells. But nobody made any reference to that night of madness, when all was so nearly lost.

9
THE BABUS OF NAYANJORE

I

Once upon a time the Babus of Nayanjore were famous landholders. They were noted for their princely extravagance. They would tear off the rough border of their Dacca muslin, because it rubbed against their skin. They could spend many thousands of rupees over the wedding of a kitten. On a certain grand occasion it is alleged that in order to turn night into day they lighted numberless lamps and showered silver threads from the sky to imitate sunlight. Those were the days before the flood. The flood came. The line of succession among these old-world Babus, with their lordly habits, could not continue for long. Like a lamp with too many wicks burning, the oil flared away quickly, and the light went out.

Kailas Babu, our neighbour, is the last relic of this extinct magnificence. Before he grew up, his family had very nearly reached its lowest ebb. When his father died, there was one dazzling outburst of funeral extravagance, and then insolvency. The property was sold to liquidate the debt. What little ready money was left over was altogether insufficient to keep up the past ancestral splendours.

Kailas Babu left Nayanjore, and came to Calcutta. His son did not remain long in this world of faded glory. He died, leaving behind him an only daughter.

In Calcutta we are Kailas Baba's neighbours. Curiously enough our own family history is just the opposite to his. My father got his money by his own exertions, and prided himself on never spending a penny more than was needed. His clothes were those of a working man, and his hands also. He never had any inclination to earn the title of Baba by extravagant display, and I myself his only son, owe him gratitude for that. He gave me the very best education, and I was able to make my way in the world. I am not ashamed of the fact that I am a self-made man.

Crisp bank-notes in my safe are dearer to me than a long pedigree in an empty family chest.

I believe this was why I disliked seeing Kailas Baba drawing his heavy cheques on the public credit from the bankrupt bank of his ancient Babu reputation I used to fancy that he looked down on me, because my father had earned money with his own hands.

I ought to have noticed that no one showed any vexation towards Kailas Babu except myself. Indeed it would have been difficult to find an old man who did less harm than he. He was always ready with his kindly little acts of courtesy in times of sorrow and joy. He would join in all the ceremonies and religious observances of his neighbours. His familiar smile would greet young and old alike. His politeness in asking details about domestic affairs was untiring. The friends who met him in the street were perforce ready to be button-holed, while a long string of questions of this kind followed one another from his lips:

"My dear friend, I am delighted to see you. Are quite well? How is Shashi? and Dada--is he all right? Do you know, I've only just heard that Madhu's son has got fever. How is he? Have you heard? And Hari Charan Babu--I've not seen him for a long time--I hope he is not ill. What's the matter with Rakkhal? And, er--er, how are the ladies of your family?"

Kailas Balm was spotlessly neat in his dress on all occasions, though his supply of clothes was sorely limited. Every day he used to air his shirts and vests and coats and trousers carefully, and put them out in the sun, along with his bed-quilt, his pillowcase, and the small carpet on which he always sat. After airing them he would shake them, and brush them, and put them on the rock. His little bits of furniture made his small room decent, and hinted that there was more in reserve if needed. Very often, for want of a servant, he would shut up his house for a while. Then he would iron out his shirts and linen with his own hands, and do other little menial tasks. After this he would open his door and receive his friends again.

Though Kailas Balm, as I have said, had lost all his landed property, he had still same family heirlooms left. There was a silver cruet for sprinkling scented water, a filigree box for otto-of-roses, a small gold salver, a costly ancient shawl, and the old-fashioned ceremonial dress and ancestral turban. These he had rescued with the greatest difficulty from the money-lenders' clutches. On every suitable occasion he would bring them out in state, and thus try to save the world-famed dignity of the Babus of Nayanjore. At heart the most modest of men, in his daily speech he regarded it as a sacred duty, owed to his rank, to give free play to his family pride. His friends would encourage this trait in his character with kindly good-humour, and it gave them great amusement.

The neighbourhood soon learnt to call him their Thakur Dada (Grandfather). They would flock to his house, and sit with him for hours together. To prevent his incurring any expense, one or other of his friends would bring him tobacco, and say: "Thakur Dada, this morning some tobacco was sent to me from Gaya. Do take it, and see how you like it."

Thakur Dada would take it, and say it was excellent. He would then go on to tell of a certain exquisite tobacco which they once smoked in the old days at Nayanjore at the cost of a guinea an ounce.

"I wonder," he used to say, "I wonder if any one would like to try it now. I have some left, and can get it at once."

Every one knew, that, if they asked for it, then somehow or other the key of the cupboard would be missing; or else Ganesh, his old family servant, had put it away somewhere.

"You never can be sure," he would add, "where things go to when servants are about. Now, this Ganesh of mine,--I can't tell you what a fool he is, but I haven't the heart to dismiss him."

Ganesh, for the credit of the family, was quite ready to bear all the blame without a word.

One of the company usually said at this point: "Never mind, Thakur Dada. Please don't trouble to look for it. This tobacco we're smoking will do quite well. The other would be too strong."

Then Thakur Dada would be relieved, and settle down again, and the talk would go on.

When his guests got up to go away, Thakur Dada would accompany them to the door, and say to them on the door-step: "Oh, by the way, when are you all coming to dine with me?"

One or other of us would answer: "Not just yet, Thakur Dada, not just yet. We'll fix a day later."

"Quite right," he would answer. "Quite right. We had much better wait till the rains come. It's too hot now. And a grand rich dinner such as I should want to give you would upset us in weather like this."

But when the rains did come, every one careful not to remind him of his promise. If the subject was brought up, some friend would suggest gently that it was very inconvenient to get about when the rains were so severe, that it would be much better to wait till they were over. And so the game went on.

His poor lodging was much too small for his position, and we used to condole with him about it. His friends would assure him they quite understood his difficulties: it was next to impossible to get a decent house in Calcutta. Indeed, they had all been looking out for years for a house to suit him, but, I need hardly add, no friend had been foolish enough to find one. Thakur Dada used to say, after a long sigh of resignation: "Well, well, I suppose I shall have to put up with this house after all." Then he would add with a genial smile: "But, you know, I could never bear to be away from my friends. I must be near you. That really compensates for everything."

Somehow I felt all this very deeply indeed. I suppose the real reason was, that when a man is young stupidity appears to him the worst of crimes. Kailas Babu was not really stupid. In ordinary business matters every one was ready to consult him.

But with regard to Nayanjore his utterances were certainly void of common sense. Because, out of amused affection for him, no one contradicted his impossible statements, he refused to keep them in bounds. When people recounted in his hearing the glorious history of Nayanjore with absurd exaggerations he would accept all they said with the utmost gravity, and never doubted, even in his dreams, that any one could disbelieve it.

II

When I sit down and try to analyse the thoughts and feelings that I had towards Kailas Babu I see that there was a still deeper reason for my dislike. I will now explain.

Though I am the son of a rich man, and might have wasted time at college, my industry was such that I took my M.A. degree in Calcutta University when quite young. My moral character was flawless. In addition, my outward appearance was so handsome, that if I were to call myself beautiful, it might be thought a mark of self-estimation, but could not be considered an untruth.

There could be no question that among the young men of Bengal I was regarded by parents generally as a very eligible match. I was myself quite clear on the point, and had determined to obtain my full value in the marriage market. When I pictured my choice, I had before my mind's eye a wealthy father's only daughter, extremely beautiful and highly educated. Proposals came pouring in to me from far and near; large sums in cash were offered. I weighed these offers with rigid impartiality, in the delicate scales of my own estimation. But there was no one fit to be my partner. I became convinced, with the poet Bhabavuti, that

In this worlds endless time and boundless space

One may be born at last to match my sovereign grace.

But in this puny modern age, and this contracted space of modern Bengal, it was doubtful if the peerless creature existed as yet.

Meanwhile my praises were sung in many tunes, and in different metres, by designing parents.

Whether I was pleased with their daughters or not, this worship which they offered was never unpleasing. I used to regard it as my proper due, because I was so good. We are told that when the gods withhold their boons from mortals they still expect their worshippers to pay them fervent honour, and are angry if it is withheld. I had that divine expectance strongly developed in myself.

I have already mentioned that Thakur Dada had an only grand-daughter. I had seen her many times, but had never mistaken her for beautiful. No thought had ever entered my mind that she would be a possible partner for myself. All the same, it seemed quite certain to me that some day ox other Kailas Babu would offer her, with all due worship, as an oblation at my shrine. Indeed-this was the secret of my dislike-I was thoroughly annoyed that he had not done it already.

I heard he had told his friends that the Babus of Nayanjore never craved a boon. Even if the girl remained unmarried, he would not break the family tradition. It was this arrogance of his that made me angry. My indignation smouldered for some time. But I remained perfectly silent, and bore it with the utmost patience, because I was so good.

As lightning accompanies thunder, so in my character a flash of humour was mingled with the mutterings of my wrath. It was, of course, impossible for me to punish the old man merely to give vent to my rage; and for a long time I did nothing at all. But suddenly one day such an amusing plan came into my head, that I could not resist the temptation of carrying it into effect.

I have already said that many of Kailas Babu's friends used to flatter the old man's vanity to the full. One, who was a retired Government servant, had told him that whenever he saw the Chota Lord Sahib he always asked for the latest news about the Babus of Nayanjore, and the Chota Lard had been heard to say that in all Bengal the only really respectable families were those of the Maharaja of Burdwan and the Babus of Nayanjore. When this monstrous falsehood was told to Kailas Balm he was extremely gratified, and often repeated the story. And wherever after that he met this Government servant in company he would ask, along with other questions:

"Oh! er--by the way, how is the Chota Lord Sahib? Quite well, did you say? Ah, yes, I am so delighted to hear it I And the dear Mem Sahib, is she quite well too? Ah, yes! and the little children-are they quite well also? Ah, yes I that's very goad news! Be sure and give them my compliments when you see them."

Kailas Balm would constantly express his intention of going some day and paying a visit to the Sahib.

But it may be taken for granted that many Chota Lords and Burro Lords also would come and go, and much water would pass down the Hoogly, before the family coach of Nayanjore would be furnished up to pay a visit to Government House.

One day I took Kailas Babu aside, and told him in a whisper: "Thakur Dada, I was at the Levee yesterday, and the Chota Lord happened to mention the Babes of Nayanjore. I told him that Kailas Balm had come to town. Do you know, he was terribly hurt because you hadn't called. He told me he was going to put etiquette on one side, and pay you a private visit himself this very afternoon."

Anybody else could have seen through this plot of mine in a moment.

And, if it had been directed against another person, Kailas Balm would have understood the joke. But after all he had heard from his friend the Government servant, and after all his own exaggerations, a visit from the Lieutenant-Governor seemed the most natural thing in the world. He became highly nervous and excited at my news. Each detail of the coming visit exercised him greatly--most of all his own ignorance of English. How on earth was that difficulty to be met? I told him there was no difficulty at all: it was aristocratic not to know English: and, besides, the Lieutenant-Governor always brought an interpreter with him, and he had expressly mentioned that this visit was to be private.

About mid-day, when most of our neighbours are at work, and the rest are asleep, a carriage and pair stopped before the lodging of Kailas Babu. Two flunkeys in livery came up the stairs, and announced in a loud voice, "The Chota Lord Sahib hoe arrived." Kailas Babu was ready, waiting for him, in his old-fashioned ceremonial robes and ancestral turban, and Ganesh was by his side, dressed in his master's best suit of clothes for the occasion. When the Chota Lord Sahib was announced, Kailas Balm ran panting and puffing and trembling to the door, and led in a friend of mine, in disguise, with repeated salaams, bowing low at each step, and walking backward as best he could. He had his old family shawl spread over a hard wooden chair, and he asked the Lord Sahib to be seated. He then made a high flown speech in Urdu, the ancient Court language of the Sahibs, and presented on the golden salver a string of gold mohurs, the last relics of his broken fortune. The old family servant Ganesh, with an expression of awe bordering on terror, stood behind with the scent-sprinkler, drenching the Lord Sahib, touching him gingerly from time to time with the otto-of-roses from the filigree box.

Kailas Babu repeatedly expressed his regret at not being able to receive His Honour Bahadur with all the ancestral magnificence of his own family estate at Nayanjore. There he could have welcomed him properly with due ceremonial. But in Calcutta he was a mere stranger and sojourner-in fact a fish out of water.

My friend, with his tall silk hat on, very gravely nodded. I need hardly say that according to English custom the hat ought to have been removed inside the room. But my friend did not dare to take it off for fear of detection; and Kailas Balm and his old servant Ganesh were sublimely unconscious of the breach of etiquette.

After a ten minutes' interview, which consisted chiefly of nodding the head, my friend rose to his feet to depart. The two flunkeys in livery, as had been planned beforehand, carried off in state the string of gold mohurs, the gold salver, the old ancestral shawl, the silver scent-sprinkler, and the otto-of-roses filigree box; they placed them ceremoniously in the carriage. Kailas Babu regarded this as the usual habit of Chota Lard Sahibs.

I was watching all the while from the next room. My sides were aching with suppressed laughter. When I could hold myself in no longer, I rushed into a further room, suddenly to discover, in a corner, a young girl sobbing as if her heart would break. When she saw my uproarious laughter she stood upright in passion, flashing the lightning of her big dark eyes in mine, and said with a tear-choked voice:

"Tell me! What harm has my grandfather done to you? Why have you come to deceive him? Why have you come here? Why--"

She could say no more. She covered her face with her hands, and broke into sobs.

My laughter vanished in a moment. It had never occurred to me that there was anything but a supremely funny joke in this act of mine, and here I discovered that I had given the cruelest pain to this tenderest little heart. All the ugliness of my cruelty rose up to condemn me. I slunk out of the room in silence, like a kicked dog.

Hitherto I had only looked upon Kusum, the grand-daughter of Kailas Babu, as a somewhat worthless commodity in the marriage market, waiting in vain to attract a husband. But now I found, with a shock of surprise, that in the corner of that room a human heart was beating.

The whole night through I had very little sleep. My mind was in a tumult. On the next day, very early in the morning, I took all those stolen goods back to Kailas Babe's lodgings, wishing to hand them over in secret to the servant Ganesh. I waited outside the door, and, not finding any one, went upstairs to Kailas Babu's room. I heard from the passage Kusum asking her grandfather in the most winning voice: "Dada, dearest, do tell me all that the Chota Lord Sahib said to you yesterday. Don't leave out a single word. I am dying to hear it all over again."

And Dada needed no encouragement. His face beamed over with pride as he related all manner of praises, which the Lard Sahib had been good enough to utter concerning the ancient families of Nayanjore. The girl was seated before him, looking up into his face, and listening with rapt attention. She was determined, out of love for the old man, to play her part to the full.

My heart was deeply touched, and tears came to my eyes. I stood there in silence in the passage, while Thakur Dada finished all his embellishments of the Chota Lord Sahib's wonderful visit. When he left the room at last, I took the stolen goods and laid them at the feet of the girl and came away without a word.

Later in the day I called again to see Kailas Balm himself. According to our ugly modern custom, I had been in the habit of making no greeting at all to this old man when I came into the room. But on this day I made a low bow, and touched his feet. I am convinced the old man thought that the coming of the Chota Lord Sahib to his house was the cause of my new politeness. He was highly gratified by it, and an air of benign severity shone from his eyes. His friends had flocked in, and he had already begun to tell again at full length the story of the Lieutenant-Governor's visit with still further adornments of a most fantastic kind. The interview was already becoming an epic, both in quality and in length.

When the other visitors had taken their leave, I made my proposal to the old man in a humble manner. I told him that, "though I could never for a moment hope to be worthy of marriage connection with such an illustrious family, yet... etc. etc."

When I made clear my proposal of marriage, the old man embraced me, and broke out in a tumult of joy: "I am a poor man, and could never have expected such great good fortune."

That was the first and last time in his life that Kailas Babu confessed to being poor. It was also the first and last time in his life that he forgot, if only for a single moment, the ancestral dignity that belongs to the Babus of Nayanjore.

10
THE KABULIWALA

My five years' old daughter Mini cannot live without chattering. I really believe that in all her life she has not wasted a minute in silence. Her mother is often vexed at this, and would stop her prattle, but I would not. To see Mini quiet is unnatural, and I cannot bear it long. And so my own talk with her is always lively.

One morning, for instance, when I was in the midst of the seventeenth chapter of my new novel, my little Mini stole into the room, and putting her hand into mine, said: "Father! Ramdayal the door-keeper calls a crow a *krow*! He doesn't know anything, does he?"

Before I could explain to her the differences of language in this world, she was embarked on the full tide of another subject. "What do you think, Father? Bhola says there is an elephant in the clouds, blowing water out of his trunk, and that is why it rains!"

And then, darting off anew, while I sat still making ready some reply to this last saying, "Father! what relation is Mother to you?"

"My dear little sister in the law!" I murmured involuntarily to myself, but with a grave face contrived to answer: "Go and play with Bhola, Mini! I am busy!"

The window of my room overlooks the road. The child had seated herself at my feet near my table, and was playing softly, drumming on her knees. I was hard at work on my seventeenth chapter, where Protrap Singh, the hero, had just caught Kanchanlata, the heroine, in his arms, and was about to escape with her by the third story window of the castle, when all of a sudden Mini left her play, and ran to the window, crying, "A kabuliwala! a kabuliwala!" Sure enough in the street below was a kabuliwala, passing slowly along. He wore the loose soiled clothing of his people, with a tall turban; there was a bag on his back, and he carried boxes of grapes in his hand.

I cannot tell what were my daughter's feelings at the sight of this man, but she began to call him loudly. "Ah!" I thought, "he will come in, and my seventeenth chapter will never be finished!" At which exact moment the Kabuliwala turned, and looked up at the child. When she saw this, overcome by terror, she fled to her mother's protection, and disappeared. She had a blind belief that inside the bag, which the big man carried, there were perhaps two or three other children like herself. The pedlar meanwhile entered my doorway, and greeted me with a smiling face.

So precarious was the position of my hero and my heroine, that my first impulse was to stop and buy something, since the man had been called. I made some small purchases, and a conversation began about Abdurrahman, the Russians, she English, and the Frontier Policy.

As he was about to leave, he asked: "And where is the little girl, sir?"

And I, thinking that Mini must get rid of her false fear, had her brought out.

She stood by my chair, and looked at the Kabuliwala and his bag. He offered her nuts and raisins, but she would not be tempted, and only clung the closer to me, with all her doubts increased.

This was their first meeting.

One morning, however, not many days later, as I was leaving the house, I was startled to find Mini, seated on a bench near the door, laughing and talking, with the great kabuliwala at her feet. In all her life, it appeared; my small daughter had never found so patient a listener, save her father. And already the corner of her little sari was stuffed with almonds and raisins, the gift of her visitor, "Why did you give her those?" I said, and taking out an eight-anna bit, I handed it to him. The man accepted the money without demur, and slipped it into his pocket.

Alas, on my return an hour later, I found the unfortunate coin had made twice its own worth of trouble! For the kabuliwala had given it to Mini, and her mother catching sight of the bright round object, had pounced on the child with: "Where did you get that eight-anna bit?"

"The Kabuliwala gave it me," said Mini cheerfully.

"The Kabuliwala gave it you!" cried her mother much shocked. "Oh, Mini! how could you take it from him?"

I, entering at the moment, saved her from impending disaster, and proceeded to make my own inquiries.

It was not the first or second time, I found, that the two had met. The kabuliwala had overcome the child's first terror by a judicious bribery of nuts and almonds, and the two were now great friends.

They had many quaint jokes, which afforded them much amusement. Seated in front of him, looking down on his gigantic frame in all her tiny dignity, Mini would ripple her face with laughter, and begin: "O kabuliwala, kabuliwala, what have you got in your bag?"

And he would reply, in the nasal accents of the mountaineer: "An elephant!" Not much cause for merriment, perhaps; but how they both enjoyed the witticism! And for me, this child's talk with a grown-up man had always in it something strangely fascinating.

Then the Kabuliwala, not to be behindhand, would take his turn: "Well, little one, and when are you going to the father-in-law's house?"

Now most small Bengali maidens have heard long ago about the father-in-law's house; but we, being a little new-fangled, had kept these things from our child, and Mini at this question must have been a trifle bewildered. But she would not show it, and with ready tact replied: "Are you going there?"

Amongst men of the Kabuliwala's class, however, it is well known that the words father-in-law's house have a double meaning. It is a euphemism for jail, the place where we are well cared for, at no expense to ourselves. In this sense would the sturdy pedlar take my daughter's question. "Ah," he would say, shaking his fist at an invisible policeman, "I will thrash my father-in-law!" Hearing this, and picturing the poor discomfited relative, Mini would go off into peals of laughter, in which her formidable friend would join.

These were autumn mornings, the very time of year when kings of old went forth to conquest; and I, never stirring from my little corner in Calcutta, would let my mind wander over the whole world. At the very name of another country, my heart would go out to it, and at the sight of a foreigner in the streets, I would fall to weaving a network of dreams,--the mountains, the glens, and the forests of his distant home, with his cottage in its setting, and the free and independent life of far-away wilds. Perhaps the scenes of travel conjure themselves up before me, and pass and repass in my imagination all the more vividly, because

I lead such a vegetable existence, that a call to travel would fall upon me like a thunderbolt. In the presence of this Kabuliwala, I was immediately transported to the foot of arid mountain peaks, with narrow little defiles twisting in and out amongst their towering heights. I could see the string of camels bearing the merchandise, and the company of turbaned merchants, carrying some of their queer old firearms, and some of their spears, journeying downward towards the plains. I could see--but at some such point Mini's mother would intervene, imploring me to "beware of that man."

Mini's mother is unfortunately a very timid lady. Whenever she hears a noise in the street, or sees people coming towards the house, she always jumps to the conclusion that they are either thieves, or drunkards, or snakes, or tigers, or malaria or cockroaches, or caterpillars, or an English sailor. Even after all these years of experience, she is not able to overcome her terror. So she was full of doubts about the Kabuliwala, and used to beg me to keep a watchful eye on him.

I tried to laugh her fear gently away, but then she would turn round on me seriously, and ask me solemn questions.

Were children never kidnapped?

Was it, then, not true that there was slavery in Cabul?

Was it so very absurd that this big man should be able to carry off a tiny child?

I urged that, though not impossible, it was highly improbable. But this was not enough, and her dread persisted. As it was indefinite, however, it did not seem right to forbid the man the house, and the intimacy went on unchecked.

Once a year in the middle of January Rahmun, the Kabuliwala, was in the habit of returning to his country, and as the time approached he would be very busy, going from house to house collecting his debts. This year, however, he could always find time to come and see Mini. It would have seemed to an outsider that there was some conspiracy between the two, for when he could not come in the morning, he would appear in the evening.

Even to me it was a little startling now and then, in the corner of a dark room, suddenly to surprise this tall, loose-garmented, much bebagged man; but when Mini would run in smiling, with her, "O!

Kabuliwala! Kabuliwala!" and the two friends, so far apart in age, would subside into their old laughter and their old jokes, I felt reassured.

One morning, a few days before he had made up his mind to go, I was correcting my proof sheets in my study. It was chilly weather. Through the window the rays of the sun touched my feet, and the slight warmth was very welcome. It was almost eight o'clock, and the early pedestrians were returning home, with their heads covered. All at once, I heard an uproar in the street, and, looking out, saw Rahmun being led away bound between two policemen, and behind them a crowd of curious boys. There were blood-stains on the clothes of the Kabuliwala, and one of the policemen carried a knife. Hurrying out, I stopped them, and enquired what it all meant. Partly from one, partly from another, I gathered that a certain neighbour had owed the pedlar something for a Rampuri shawl, but had falsely denied having bought it, and that in the course of the quarrel, Rahmun had struck him. Now in the heat of his excitement, the prisoner began calling his enemy all sorts of names, when suddenly in a verandah of my house appeared my little Mini, with her usual exclamation: "O Kabuliwala! Kabuliwala!" Rahmun's face lighted up as he turned to her. He had no bag under his arm today, so she could not discuss the elephant with him. She at once therefore proceeded to the next question: "Are you going to the father-in-law's house?" Rahmun laughed and said: "Just where I am going, little one!" Then seeing that the reply did not amuse the child, he held up his fettered hands. "Ali," he said, "I would have thrashed that old father-in-law, but my hands are bound!"

On a charge of murderous assault, Rahmun was sentenced to some years' imprisonment.

Time passed away, and he was not remembered. The accustomed work in the accustomed place was ours, and the thought of the once-free mountaineer spending his years in prison seldom or never occurred to us. Even my light-hearted Mini, I am ashamed to say, forgot her old friend. New companions filled her life. As she grew older, she spent more of her time with girls. So much time indeed did she spend with them that she came no more, as she used to do, to her father's room. I was scarcely on speaking terms with her.

Years had passed away. It was once more autumn and we had made arrangements for our Mini's marriage. It was to take place during the Puja Holidays. With Durga returning to Kailas, the light of our home also was to depart to her husband's house, and leave her father's in the shadow.

The morning was bright. After the rains, there was a sense of ablution in the air, and the sun-rays looked like pure gold. So bright were they that they gave a beautiful radiance even to the sordid brick walls of our Calcutta lanes. Since early dawn to-day the wedding-pipes had been sounding, and at each beat my own heart throbbed. The wail of the tune, Bhairavi, seemed to intensify my pain at the approaching separation. My Mini was to be married to-night.

From early morning noise and bustle had pervaded the house. In the courtyard the canopy had to be slung on its bamboo poles; the chandeliers with their tinkling sound must be hung in each room and verandah. There was no end of hurry and excitement. I was sitting in my study, looking through the accounts, when some one entered, saluting respectfully, and stood before me. It was Rahmun the Kabuliwala. At first I did not recognise him. He had no bag, nor the long hair, nor the same vigour that he used to have. But he smiled, and I knew him again.

"When did you come, Rahmun?" I asked him.

"Last evening," he said, "I was released from jail."

The words struck harsh upon my ears. I had never before talked with one who had wounded his fellow, and my heart shrank within itself, when I realised this, for I felt that the day would have been better-omened had he not turned up.

"There are ceremonies going on," I said, "and I am busy. Could you perhaps come another day?"

At once he turned to go; but as he reached the door he hesitated, and said: "May I not see the little one, sir, for a moment?" It was his belief that Mini was still the same. He had pictured her running to him as she used, calling "O Kabuliwala! Kabuliwala!" He had imagined too that they would laugh and talk together, just as of old. In fact, in memory of former days he had brought, carefully wrapped up in paper, a few almonds and raisins and grapes, obtained somehow from a countryman, for his own little fund was dispersed.

I said again: "There is a ceremony in the house, and you will not be able to see any one to-day."

The man's face fell. He looked wistfully at me for a moment, said "Good morning," and went out. I felt a little sorry, and would have called him back, but I found he was returning of his own accord. He came close up to me holding out his offerings and said: "I brought these few things, sir, for the little one. Will you give them to her?"

I took them and was going to pay him, but he caught my hand and said: "You are very kind, sir! Keep me in your recollection. Do not offer me money!--You have a little girl, I too have one like her in my own home. I think of her, and bring fruits to your child, not to make a profit for myself."

Saying this, he put his hand inside his big loose robe, and brought out a small and dirty piece of paper. With great care he unfolded this, and smoothed it out with both hands on my table. It bore the impression of a little band. Not a photograph. Not a drawing. The impression of an ink-smeared hand laid flat on the paper. This touch of his own little daughter had been always on his heart, as he had come year after year to Calcutta, to sell his wares in the streets.

Tears came to my eyes. I forgot that he was a poor Cabuli fruit-seller, while I was--but no, what was I more than he? He also was a father. That impression of the hand of his little Parbati in her distant mountain home reminded me of my own little Mini.

I sent for Mini immediately from the inner apartment. Many difficulties were raised, but I would not listen. Clad in the red silk of her wedding-day, with the sandal paste on her forehead, and adorned as a young bride, Mini came, and stood bashfully before me.

The Kabuliwala looked a little staggered at the apparition. He could not revive their old friendship. At last he smiled and said: "Little one, are you going to your father-in-law's house?"

But Mini now understood the meaning of the word "father-in-law," and she could not reply to him as of old. She flushed up at the question, and stood before him with her bride-like face turned down.

I remembered the day when the Kabuliwala and my Mini had first met, and I felt sad. When she had gone, Rahmun heaved a deep sigh, and sat down on the floor. The idea had suddenly come to him that his daughter too must have grown in this long time, and that he would have to make friends with her anew. Assuredly he would not find her, as he used to know her. And besides, what might not have happened to her in these eight years?

The marriage-pipes sounded, and the mild autumn sun streamed round us. But Rahmun sat in the little Calcutta lane, and saw before him the barren mountains of Afghanistan.

I took out a bank-note, and gave it to him, saying: "Go back to your own daughter, Rahmun, in your own country, and may the happiness of your meeting bring good fortune to my child!"

Having made this present, I had to curtail some of the festivities. I could not have the electric lights I had intended, nor the military band, and the ladies of the house were despondent at it. But to me the wedding feast was all the brighter for the thought that in a distant land a long-lost father met again with his only child.

11
THE POSTMASTER

The postmaster first took up his duties in the village of Ulapur. Though the village was a small one, there was an indigo factory near by, and the proprietor, an Englishman, had managed to get a post office established.

Our postmaster belonged to Calcutta. He felt like a fish out of water in this remote village. His office and living-room were in a dark thatched shed, not far from a green, slimy pond, surrounded on all sides by a dense growth.

The men employed in the indigo factory had no leisure; moreover, they were hardly desirable companions for decent folk. Nor is a Calcutta boy an adept in the art of associating with others. Among strangers he appears either proud or ill at ease. At any rate, the postmaster had but little company; nor had he much to do.

At times he tried his hand at writing a verse or two. That the movement of the leaves and the clouds of the sky were enough to fill life with joy— such were the sentiments to which he sought to give expression. But God knows that the poor fellow would have felt it as the gift of a new life, if some genie of the Arabian Nights had in one night swept away the trees, leaves and all, and replaced them with a macadamised road, hiding the clouds from view with rows of tall houses.

The postmaster's salary was small. He had to cook his own meals, which he used to share with Ratan, an orphan girl of the village, who did odd jobs for him.

When in the evening the smoke began to curl up from the village cowsheds, and the cicalas chirped in every bush; when the mendicants of the Baül sect sang their shrill songs in their daily meeting-place, when any poet, who had attempted to watch the movement of the leaves in the dense bamboo thickets, would have felt a ghostly shiver run down his back, the postmaster would light his little lamp, and call out "Ratan."

Ratan would sit outside waiting for this call, and, instead of coming in at once, would reply, "Did you call me, sir?"

"What are you doing?" the postmaster would ask.

"I must be going to light the kitchen fire," would be the answer.

And the postmaster would say: "Oh, let the kitchen fire be for awhile; light me my pipe first."

At last Ratan would enter, with puffed-out cheeks, vigorously blowing into a flame a live coal to light the tobacco. This would give the postmaster an opportunity of conversing. "Well, Ratan," perhaps he would begin, "do you remember anything of your mother?" That was a fertile subject. Ratan partly remembered, and partly didn't. Her father had been fonder of her than her mother; him she recollected more vividly. He used to come home in the evening after his work, and one or two evenings stood out more clearly than others, like pictures in her memory. Ratan would sit on the floor near the postmaster's feet, as memories crowded in upon her. She called to mind a little brother that she had—and how on some bygone cloudy day she had played at fishing with him on the edge of the pond, with a twig for a make-believe fishing-rod. Such little incidents would drive out greater events from her mind. Thus, as they talked, it would often get very late, and the postmaster would feel too lazy to do any cooking at all. Ratan would then hastily light the fire, and toast some unleavened bread, which, with the cold remnants of the morning meal, was enough for their supper.

On some evenings, seated at his desk in the corner of the big empty shed, the postmaster too would call up memories of his own home, of his mother and his sister, of those for whom in his exile his heart was sad,—memories which were always haunting him, but which he could not talk about with the men of the factory, though he found himself naturally recalling them aloud in the presence of the simple little girl. And so it came about that the girl would allude to his people as mother, brother, and sister, as if she had known them all her life. In fact, she had a complete picture of each one of them painted in her little heart.

One noon, during a break in the rains, there was a cool soft breeze blowing; the smell of the damp grass and leaves in the hot sun felt like the warm breathing of the tired earth on one's body. A persistent bird went on all the afternoon repeating the burden of its one complaint in Nature's audience chamber.

The postmaster had nothing to do. The shimmer of the freshly washed leaves, and the banked-up remnants of the retreating rain-clouds were sights to see; and the postmaster was watching them and thinking to himself: "Oh, if only some kindred soul were near—just one loving human being whom I could hold near my heart!" This was exactly, he went on to think, what that bird was trying to say, and it was the same feeling which the murmuring leaves were striving to express. But no one knows, or would believe, that such an idea might also take possession of an ill-paid village postmaster in the deep, silent mid-day interval of his work.

The postmaster sighed, and called out "Ratan." Ratan was then sprawling beneath the guava-tree, busily engaged in eating unripe guavas. At the voice of her master, she ran up breathlessly, saying: "Were you calling me, Dada?" "I was thinking," said the postmaster, "of teaching you to read." And then for the rest of the afternoon he taught her the alphabet.

Thus, in a very short time, Ratan had got as far as the double consonants.

It seemed as though the showers of the season would never end. Canals, ditches, and hollows were all overflowing with water. Day and night the patter of rain was heard, and the croaking of frogs. The village roads became impassable, and marketing had to be done in punts.

One heavily clouded morning, the postmaster's little pupil had been long waiting outside the door for her call, but, not hearing it as usual, she took up her dog-eared book, and slowly entered the room. She found her master stretched out on his bed, and, thinking that he was resting, she was about to retire on tip-toe, when she suddenly heard her name—"Ratan!" She turned at once and asked: "Were you sleeping, Dada?" The postmaster in a plaintive voice said: "I am not well. Feel my head; is it very hot?"

In the loneliness of his exile, and in the gloom of the rains, his ailing body needed a little tender nursing. He longed to remember the touch on the forehead of soft hands with tinkling bracelets, to imagine the presence of loving womanhood, the nearness of mother and sister. And the exile was not disappointed. Ratan ceased to be a little girl. She at once stepped into the post of mother, called in the village doctor, gave the patient his pills at the proper intervals, sat up all night by his pillow, cooked his gruel for him, and every now and then asked: "Are you feeling a little better, Dada?"

It was some time before the postmaster, with weakened body, was able to leave his sick-bed. "No more of this," said he with decision. "I must get a transfer." He at once wrote off to Calcutta an application for a transfer, on the ground of the unhealthiness of the place.

Relieved from her duties as nurse, Ratan again took up her old place outside the door. But she no longer heard the same old call. She would sometimes peep inside furtively to find the postmaster sitting on his chair, or stretched on his bed, and staring absent-mindedly into the air. While Ratan was awaiting her call, the postmaster was awaiting a reply to his application. The girl read her old lessons over and over again,— her great fear was lest, when the call came, she might be found wanting in the double consonants. At last, after a week, the call did come one evening. With an overflowing heart Ratan rushed into the room with her—"Were you calling me, Dada?"

The postmaster said: "I am going away to-morrow, Ratan."

"Where are you going, Dada?"

"I am going home."

"When will you come back?"

"I am not coming back."

Ratan asked no other question. The postmaster, of his own accord, went on to tell her that his application for a transfer had been rejected, so he had resigned his post and was going home.

For a long time neither of them spoke another word. The lamp went on dimly burning, and from a leak in one corner of the thatch water dripped steadily into an earthen vessel on the floor beneath it.

After a while Ratan rose, and went off to the kitchen to prepare the meal; but she was not so quick about it as on other days. Many new things to think of had entered her little brain. When the postmaster had finished his supper, the girl suddenly asked him: "Dada, will you take me to your home?"

The postmaster laughed. "What an idea!" said he; but he did not think it necessary to explain to the girl wherein lay the absurdity.

That whole night, in her waking and in her dreams, the postmaster's laughing reply haunted her—"What an idea!"

On getting up in the morning, the postmaster found his bath ready. He had stuck to his Calcutta habit of bathing in water drawn and kept in pitchers, instead of taking a plunge in the river as was the custom of the village. For some reason or other, the girl could not ask him about the time of his departure, so she had fetched the water from the river long before sunrise, that it should be ready as early as he might want it. After the bath came a call for Ratan. She entered noiselessly, and looked silently into her master's face for orders. The master said: "You need not be anxious about my going away, Ratan; I shall tell my successor to look after you." These words were kindly meant, no doubt: but inscrutable are the ways of a woman's heart!

Ratan had borne many a scolding from her master without complaint, but these kind words she could not bear. She burst out weeping, and said: "No, no, you need not tell anybody anything at all about me; I don't want to stay on here."

The postmaster was dumbfounded. He had never seen Ratan like this before.

The new incumbent duly arrived, and the postmaster, having given over charge, prepared to depart. Just before starting he called Ratan and said: "Here is something for you; I hope it will keep you for some little time." He brought out from his pocket the whole of his month's salary, retaining only a trifle for his travelling expenses. Then Ratan fell at his feet and cried: "Oh, Dada, I pray you, don't give me anything, don't in any way trouble about me," and then she ran away out of sight.

The postmaster heaved a sigh, took up his carpet bag, put his umbrella over his shoulder, and, accompanied by a man carrying his many-coloured tin trunk, he slowly made for the boat.

When he got in and the boat was under way, and the rain-swollen river, like a stream of tears welling up from the earth, swirled and sobbed at her bows, then he felt a pain at heart; the grief-stricken face of a village girl seemed to represent for him the great unspoken pervading grief of Mother Earth herself. At one time he had an impulse to go back, and bring away along with him that lonesome waif, forsaken of the world. But the wind had just filled the sails, the boat had got well into the middle of the turbulent current, and already the village was left behind, and its outlying burning-ground came in sight.

So the traveller, borne on the breast of the swift-flowing river, consoled himself with philosophical reflections on the numberless meetings and partings going on in the world—on death, the great parting, from which none returns.

But Ratan had no philosophy. She was wandering about the post office in a flood of tears. It may be that she had still a lurking hope in some corner of her heart that her Dada would return, and that is why she could not tear herself away. Alas for our foolish human nature! Its fond mistakes are persistent. The dictates of reason take a long time to assert their own sway. The surest proofs meanwhile are disbelieved. False hope is clung to with all one's might and main, till a day comes when it has sucked the heart dry and it forcibly breaks through its bonds and departs. After that comes the misery of awakening, and then once again the longing to get back into the maze of the same mistakes.

12
THE POST OFFICE
ACT I

[Madhav's House]

Madhav. What a state I am in! Before he came, nothing mattered; I felt so free. But now that he has come, goodness knows from where, my heart is filled with his dear self, and my home will be no home to me when he leaves. Doctor, do you think he--

Physician. If there's life in his fate, then he will live long. But what the medical scriptures say, it seems--

Madhav. Great heavens, what?

Physician. The scriptures have it: "Bile or palsey, cold or gout spring all alike."

Madhav. Oh, get along, don't fling your scriptures at me; you only make me more anxious; tell me what I can do.

Physician. [Taking snuff] The patient needs the most scrupulous care.

Madhav. That's true; but tell me how.

Physician. I have already mentioned, on no account must he be let out of doors.

Madhav. Poor child, it is very hard to keep him indoors all day long.

Physician. What else can you do? The autumn sun and the damp are both very bad for the little fellow--for the scriptures have it:
"In wheezing, swoon or in nervous fret,
In jaundice or leaden eyes--"

Madhav. Never mind the scriptures, please. Eh, then we must shut the poor thing up. Is there no other method?

	Physician. None at all: for, "In the wind and in the sun--"
Madhav.	What will your "in this and in that" do for me now? Why don't you let them alone and come straight to the point? What's to be done then? Your system is very, very hard for the poor boy; and he is so quiet too with all his pain and sickness. It tears my heart to see him wince, as he takes your medicine.
Physician.	Effect. That's why the sage Chyabana observes: "In medicine as in good advices, the least palatable ones are the truest." Ah, well! I must be trotting now.

[Exit]

[Gaffer Enters]

Madhav.	Well, I'm jiggered, there's Gaffer now.
Gaffer.	Why, why, I won't bite you.
Madhav.	No, but you are a devil to send children off their heads.
Gaffer.	But you aren't a child, and you've no child in the house; why worry then?
Madhav.	Oh, but I have brought a child into the house.
Gaffer.	Indeed, how so?
Madhav.	You remember how my wife was dying to adopt a child?
Gaffer.	Yes, but that's an old story; you didn't like the idea.
Madhav.	You know, brother, how hard all this getting money in has been. That somebody else's child would sail in and waste all this money earned with so much trouble--Oh, I hated the idea. But this boy clings to my heart in such a queer sort of way--
Gaffer.	So that's the trouble! and your money goes all for him and feels jolly lucky it does go at all.
Madhav.	Formerly, earning was a sort of passion with me; I simply couldn't help working for money. Now, I make money and as I know it is all for this dear boy, earning becomes a joy to me.
Gaffer.	Ah, well, and where did you pick him up?
Madhav.	He is the son of a man who was a brother to my wife by village ties. He has had no mother since infancy; and now the other day he lost his father as well.

Gaffer.	Poor thing: and so he needs me all the more.
Madhav.	The doctor says all the organs of his little body are at loggerheads with each other, and there isn't much hope for his life. There is only one way to save him and that is to keep him out of this autumn wind and sun. But you are such a terror! What with this game of yours at your age, too, to get children out of doors!
Gaffer.	God bless my soul! So I'm already as bad as autumn wind and sun, eh! But, friend, I know something, too, of the game of keeping them indoors. When my day's work is over I am coming in to make friends with this child of yours.

[Exit]

[Amal enters]

Amal.	Uncle, I say, Uncle!
Madhav.	Hullo! Is that you, Amal?
Amal.	Mayn't I be out of the courtyard at all?
Madhav.	No, my dear, no.
Amal.	See, there where Auntie grinds lentils in the quirn, the squirrel is sitting with his tail up and with his wee hands he's picking up the broken grains of lentilsand crunching them. Can't I run up there?
Madhav.	No, my darling, no.
Amal.	Wish I were a squirrel!--it would be lovely. Uncle, why won't you let me go about?
Madhav.	Doctor says it's bad for you to be out.
Amal.	How can the doctor know?
Madhav.	What a thing to say! The doctor can't know and he reads such huge books!
Amal.	Does his book-learning tell him everything?
Madhav.	Of course, don't you know!
Amal.	[With a sigh] Ah, I am so stupid! I don't read books.
Madhav.	Now, think of it; very, very learned people are all like you; they are never out of doors.
Amal.	Aren't they really?
Madhav.	No, how can they? Early and late they toil and moil at

their books, and they've eyes for nothing else. Now, my little man, you are going to be learned when you grow up; and then you will stay at home and read such big books, and people will notice you and say, "he's a wonder."

Amal.   No, no, Uncle; I beg of you by your dear feet--I don't want to be learned, I won't.

Madhav.   Dear, dear; it would have been my saving if I could have been learned.

Amal.   No, I would rather go about and see everything that there is.

Madhav.   Listen to that! See! What will you see, what is there so much to see?

Amal.   See that far-away hill from our window--I often long to go beyond those hills and right away.

Madhav.   Oh, you silly! As if there's nothing more to be done but just get up to the top of that hill and away! Eh! You don't talk sense, my boy. Now listen, since that hill stands there upright as a barrier, it means you can't get beyond it. Else, what was the use in heaping up so many large stones to make such a big affair of it, eh!

Amal.   Uncle, do you think it is meant to prevent your crossing over? It seems to me because the earth can't speak it raises its hands into the sky and beckons. And those who live far and sit alone by their windows can see the signal. But I suppose the learned people--

Madhav.   No, they don't have time for that sort of nonsense. They are not crazy like you.

Amal.   Do you know, yesterday I met someone quite as crazy as I am.

Madhav.   Gracious me, really, how so?

Amal.   He had a bamboo staff on his shoulder with a small bundle at the top, and a brass pot in his left hand, and an old pair of shoes on; he was making for those hills straight across that meadow there. I called out to him and asked, "Where are you going?" He answered,

"I don't know, anywhere!" I asked again, "Why are you going?" He said, "I'm going out to seek work." Say, Uncle, have you to seek work?

Madhav.   Of course I have to. There's many about looking for jobs.

Amal.   How lovely! I'll go about, like them too, finding things to do.

Madhav.   Suppose you seek and don't find. Then--

Amal.   Wouldn't that be jolly? Then I should go farther! I watched that man slowly walking on with his pair of worn out shoes. And when he got to where the water flows under the fig tree, he stopped and washed his feet in the stream. Then he took out from his bundle some gram-flour, moistened it with water and began to eat. Then he tied up his bundle and shouldered it again; tucked up his cloth above his knees and crossed the stream. I've asked Auntie to let me go up to the stream, and eat my gram-flour just like him.

Madhav.   And what did your Auntie say to that?

Amal.   Auntie said, "Get well and then I'll take you over there." Please, Uncle, when shall I get well?

Madhav.   It won't be long, dear.

Amal.   Really, but then I shall go right away the moment I'm well again.

Madhav.   And where will you go?

Amal.   Oh, I will walk on, crossing so many streams, wading through water. Everybody will be asleep with their doors shut in the heat of the day and I will tramp on and on seeking work far, very far.

Madhav.   I see! I think you had better be getting well first; then--

Amal.   But then you won't want me to be learned, will you, Uncle?

Madhav.   What would you rather be then?

Amal.   I can't think of anything just now; but I'll tell you later on.

Madhav.   Very well. But mind you, you aren't to call out and talk to strangers again.

Amal.	But I love to talk to strangers!
Madhav.	Suppose they had kidnapped you?
Amal.	That would have been splendid! But no one ever takes me away. They all want me to stay in here.
Madhav.	I am off to my work--but, darling, you won't go out, will you?
Amal.	No, I won't. But, Uncle, you'll let me be in this room by the roadside.

[Exit Madhav]

Dairyman.	Curds, curds, good nice curds.
Amal.	Curdseller, I say, Curdseller.
Dairyman.	Why do you call me? Will you buy some curds?
Amal.	How can I buy? I have no money.
Dairyman.	What a boy! Why call out then? Ugh! What a waste of time.
Amal.	I would go with you if I could.
Dairyman.	With me?
Amal.	Yes, I seem to feel homesick when I hear you call from far down the road.
Dairyman.	[Lowering his yoke-pole] Whatever are you doing here, my child?
Amal.	The doctor says I'm not to be out, so I sit here all day long.
Dairyman.	My poor child, whatever has happened to you?
Amal.	I can't tell. You see I am not learned, so I don't know what's the matter with me. Say, Dairyman, where do you come from?
Dairyman.	From our village.
Amal.	Your village? Is it very far?
Dairyman.	Our village lies on the river Shamli at the foot of the Panch-mura hills.
Amal.	Panch-mura hills! Shamli river! I wonder. I may have seen your village. I can't think when though!
Dairyman.	Have you seen it? Been to the foot of those hills?
Amal.	Never. But I seem to remember having seen it. Your

	village is under some very old big trees, just by the side of the red road--isn't that so?
Dairyman.	That's right, child.
Amal.	And on the slope of the hill cattle grazing.
Dairyman.	How wonderful! Aren't there cattle grazing in our village! Indeed, there are!
Amal.	And your women with red *sarees* fill their pitchers from the river and carry them on their heads.
Dairyman.	Good, that's right. Women from our dairy village do come and draw their water from the river; but then it isn't everyone who has a red *saree* to put on. But, my dear child, surely you must have been there for a walk some time.
Amal.	Really, Dairyman, never been there at all. But the first day doctor lets me go out, you are going to take me to your village.
Dairyman.	I will, my child, with pleasure.
Amal.	And you'll teach me to cry curds and shoulder the yoke like you and walk the long, long road?
Dairyman.	Dear, dear, did you ever? Why should you sell curds? No, you will read big books and be learned.
Amal.	No, I never want to be learned--I'll be like you and take my curds from the village by the red road near the old banyan tree, and I will hawk it from cottage to cottage. Oh, how do you cry--"Curd, curd, good nice curd!" Teach me the tune, will you?
Dairyman.	Dear, dear, teach you the tune; what an idea!
Amal.	Please do. I love to hear it. I can't tell you how queer I feel when I hear you cry out from the bend of that road, through the line of those trees! Do you know I feel like that when I hear the shrill cry of kites from almost the end of the sky?
Dairyman.	Dear child, will you have some curds? Yes, do.
Amal.	But I have no money.
Dairyman.	No, no, no, don't talk of money! You'll make me so happy if you have a little curds from me.

Amal.	Say, have I kept you too long?
Dairyman.	Not a bit; it has been no loss to me at all; you have taught me how to be happy selling curds.

[Exit]

Amal.	[Intoning] Curds, curds, good nice curds--from the dairy village--from the country of the Panch-mura hills by the Shamli bank. Curds, good curds; in the early morning the women make the cows stand in a row under the trees and milk them, and in the evening they turn the milk into curds. Curds, good curds. Hello, there's the watchman on his rounds. Watchman, I say, come and have a word with me.
Watchman.	What's all this row you are making? Aren't you afraid of the likes of me?
Amal.	No, why should I be?
Watchman.	Suppose I march you off then?
Amal.	Where will you take me to? Is it very far, right beyond the hills?
Watchman.	Suppose I march you straight to the King?
Amal.	To the King! Do, will you? But the doctor won't let me go out. No one can ever take me away. I've got to stay here all day long.
Watchman.	Doctor won't let you, poor fellow! So I see! Your face is pale and there are dark rings round your eyes. Your veins stick out from your poor thin hands.
Amal.	Won't you sound the gong, Watchman?
Watchman.	Time has not yet come.
Amal.	How curious! Some say time has not yet come, and some say time has gone by! But surely your time will come the moment you strike the gong!
Watchman.	That's not possible; I strike up the gong only when it is time.
Amal.	Yes, I love to hear your gong. When it is midday and our meal is over, Uncle goes off to his work and Auntie falls asleep reading her Ramayana, and in the courtyard under the shadow of the wall our doggie sleeps with

his nose in his curled up tail; then your gong strikes out, "Dong, dong, dong!" Tell me why does your gong sound?

Watchman. My gong sounds to tell the people, Time waits for none, but goes on forever.

Amal. Where, to what land?

Watchman. That none knows.

Amal. Then I suppose no one has ever been there! Oh, I do wish to fly with the time to that land of which no one knows anything.

Watchman. All of us have to get there one day, my child.

Amal. Have I too?

Watchman. Yes, you too!

Amal. But doctor won't let me out.

Watchman. One day the doctor himself may take you there by the hand.

Amal. He won't; you don't know him. He only keeps me in.

Watchman. One greater than he comes and lets us free.

Amal. When will this great doctor come for me? I can't stick in here any more.

Watchman. Shouldn't talk like that, my child.

Amal. No. I am here where they have left me--I never move a bit. But when your gong goes off, dong, dong, dong, it goes to my heart. Say, Watchman?

Watchman. Yes, my dear.

Amal. Say, what's going on there in that big house on the other side, where there is a flag flying high up and the people are always going in and out?

Watchman. Oh, there? That's our new Post Office.

Amal. Post Office? Whose?

Watchman. Whose? Why, the King's surely!

Amal. Do letters come from the King to his office here?

Watchman. Of course. One fine day there may be a letter for you in there.

Amal. A letter for me? But I am only a little boy.

Watchman. The King sends tiny notes to little boys.

Amal.	Oh, how lovely! When shall I have my letter? How do you guess he'll write to me?
Watchman.	Otherwise why should he set his Post Office here right in front of your open window, with the golden flag flying?
Amal.	But who will fetch me my King's letter when it comes?
Watchman.	The King has many postmen. Don't you see them run about with round gilt badges on their chests?
Amal.	Well, where do they go?
Watchman.	Oh, from door to door, all through the country.
Amal.	I'll be the King's postman when I grow up.
Watchman.	Ha! ha! Postman, indeed! Rain or shine, rich or poor, from house to house delivering letters--that's very great work!
Amal.	That's what I'd like best. What makes you smile so? Oh, yes, your work is great too. When it is silent everywhere in the heat of the noonday, your gong sounds, Dong, dong, dong,-- and sometimes when I wake up at night all of a sudden and find our lamp blown out, I can hear through the darkness your gong slowly sounding, Dong, dong, dong!
Watchman.	There's the village headman! I must be off. If he catches me gossiping with you there'll be a great to do.
Amal.	The headman? Whereabouts is he?
Watchman.	Right down the road there; see that huge palm-leaf umbrella hopping along? That's him!
Amal.	I suppose the King's made him our headman here?
Watchman.	Made him? Oh, no! A fussy busy-body! He knows so many ways of making himself unpleasant that everybody is afraid of him. It's just a game for the likes of him, making trouble for everybody. I must be off now! Mustn't keep work waiting, you know! I'll drop in again to-morrow morning and tell you all the news of the town.
	[Exit]
Amal.	It would be splendid to have a letter from the King

every day. I'll read them at the window. But, oh! I can't read writing. Who'll read them out to me, I wonder! Auntie reads her Ramayana; she may know the King's writing. If no one will, then I must keep them carefully and read them when I'm grown up. But if the postman can't find me? Headman, Mr. Headman, may I have a word with you?

Headman.   Who is yelling after me on the highway? Oh, you wretched monkey!

Amal.   You're the headman. Everybody minds you.

Headman.   [Looking pleased] Yes, oh yes, they do! They must!

Amal.   Do the King's postmen listen to you?

Headman.   They've got to. By Jove, I'd like to see--

Amal.   Will you tell the postman it's Amal who sits by the window here?

Headman.   What's the good of that?

Amal.   In case there's a letter for me.

Headman.   A letter for you! Whoever's going to write to you?

Amal.   If the King does.

Headman.   Ha! ha! What an uncommon little fellow you are! Ha! ha! the King indeed, aren't you his bosom friend, eh! You haven't met for a long while and the King is pining, I am sure. Wait till to-morrow and you'll have your letter.

Amal.   Say, Headman, why do you speak to me in that tone of voice? Are you cross?

Headman.   Upon my word! Cross, indeed! You write to the King! Madhav is devilish swell nowadays. He'd made a little pile; and so kings and padishahs are everyday talk with his people. Let me find him once and I'll make him dance. Oh, you snipper-snapper! I'll get the King's letter sent to your house--indeed I will!

Amal.   No, no, please don't trouble yourself about it.

Headman.   And why not, pray! I'll tell the King about you and he won't be very long. One of his footmen will come along presently for news of you. Madhav's impudence staggers me. If the King hears of this, that'll take some of his nonsense out of him.

[Exit]

Amal.   Who are you walking there? How your anklets tinkle! Do stop a while, dear, won't you?

[A Girl Enters]

Girl.   I haven't a moment to spare; it is already late!

Amal.   I see, you don't wish to stop; I don't care to stay on here either.

Girl.   You make me think of some late star of the morning! Whatever's the matter with you?

Amal.   I don't know; the doctor won't let me out.

Girl.   Ah me! Don't then! Should listen to the doctor. People'll be cross with you if you're naughty. I know, always looking out and watching must make you feel tired. Let me close the window a bit for you.

Amal.   No, don't, only this one's open! All the others are shut. But will you tell me who you are? Don't seem to know you.

Girl.   I am Sudha.

Amal.   What Sudha?

Sudha.   Don't you know? Daughter of the flower-seller here.

Amal.   What do you do?

Sudha.   I gather flowers in my basket.

Amal.   Oh, flower gathering! That is why your feet seem so glad and your anklets jingle so merrily as you walk. Wish I could be out too. Then I would pick some flowers for you from the very topmost branches right out of sight.

Sudha.   Would you really? Do you know more about flowers than I?

Amal.   Yes, I do, quite as much. I know all about Champa of the fairy tale and his seven brothers. If only they let me, I'll go right into the dense forest where you can't find your way. And where the honey-sipping hummingbird rocks himself on the end of the thinnest branch, I will

	flower out as a champa. Would you be my sister Parul?
Sudha.	You are silly! How can I be sister Parul when I am Sudha and my mother is Sasi, the flower-seller? I have to weave so many garlands a day. It would be jolly if I could lounge here like you!
Amal.	What would you do then, all the day long?
Sudha.	I could have great times with my doll Benay the bride, and Meni the pussycat and--but I say it is getting late and I mustn't stop, or I won't find a single flower.
Amal.	Oh, wait a little longer; I do like it so!
Sudha.	Ah, well--now don't you be naughty. Be good and sit still and on my way back home with the flowers I'll come and talk with you.
Amal.	And you'll let me have a flower then?
Sudha.	No, how can I? It has to be paid for.
Amal.	I'll pay when I grow up--before I leave to look for work out on the other side of that stream there.
Sudha.	Very well, then.
Amal.	And you'll come back when you have your flowers?
Sudha.	I will.
Amal.	You will, really?
Sudha.	Yes, I will.
Amal.	You won't forget me? I am Amal, remember that.
Sudha.	I won't forget you, you'll see.

[Exit]

[A Troop of Boys Enter]

Amal.	Say, brothers, where are you all off to? Stop here a little.
Boys.	We're off to play.
Amal.	What will you play at, brothers?
Boys.	We'll play at being ploughmen.
First Boy.	[Showing a stick] This is our ploughshare.
Second Boy.	We two are the pair of oxen.
Amal.	And you're going to play the whole day?
Boys.	Yes, all day long.
Amal.	And you'll come back home in the evening by the road along the river bank?

Boys.	Yes.
Amal.	Do you pass our house on your way home?
Boys.	You come out to play with us, yes do.
Amal.	Doctor won't let me out.
Boys.	Doctor! Suppose the likes of you mind the doctor. Let's be off; it is getting late.
Amal.	Don't. Why not play on the road near this window? I could watch you then.
Third Boy.	What can we play at here?
Amal.	With all these toys of mine lying about. Here you are, have them. I can't play alone. They are getting dirty and are of no use to me.
Boys.	How jolly! What fine toys! Look, here's a ship. There's old mother Jatai; say, chaps, ain't he a gorgeous sepoy? And you'll let us have them all? You don't really mind?
Amal.	No, not a bit; have them by all means.
Boys.	You don't want them back?
Amal.	Oh, no, I shan't want them.
Boys.	Say, won't you get a scolding for this?
Amal.	No one will scold me. But will you play with them in front of our door for a while every morning? I'll get you new ones when these are old.
Boys.	Oh, yes, we will. Say, chaps, put these sepoys into a line. We'll play at war; where can we get a musket? Oh, look here, this bit of reed will do nicely. Say, but you're off to sleep already.
Amal.	I'm afraid I'm sleepy. I don't know, I feel like it at times. I have been sitting a long while and I'm tired; my back aches.
Boys.	It's only early noon now. How is it you're sleepy? Listen! The gong's sounding the first watch.
Amal.	Yes, dong, dong, dong, it tolls me to sleep.
Boys.	We had better go then. We'll come in again to-morrow morning.
Amal.	I want to ask you something before you go. You are always out--do you know of the King's postmen?

Boys.	Yes, quite well.
Amal.	Who are they? Tell me their names.
Boys.	One's Badal, another's Sarat. There's so many of them.
Amal.	Do you think they will know me if there's a letter for me?
Boys.	Surely, if your name's on the letter they will find you out.
Amal.	When you call in to-morrow morning, will you bring one of them along so that he'll know me?
	Boys Yes, if you like.

Curtain

ACT II

[Amal in Bed]

Amal.   Can't I go near the window to-day, Uncle? Would the doctor mind that too?

Madhav.   Yes, darling, you see you've made yourself worse squatting there day after day.

Amal.   Oh, no, I don't know if it's made me more ill, but I always feel well when I'm there.

Madhav.   No, you don't; you squat there and make friends with the whole lot of people round here, old and young, as if they are holding a fair right under my eaves--flesh and blood won't stand that strain. Just see--your face is quite pale.

Amal.   Uncle, I fear my fakir'll pass and not see me by the window.

Madhav.   Your fakir, whoever's that?

Amal.   He comes and chats to me of the many lands where he's been. I love to hear him.

Madhav.   How's that? I don't know of any fakirs.

Amal.   This is about the time he comes in. I beg of you, by your dear feet, ask him in for a moment to talk to me here. *[Gaffer Enters in a Fakir's Guise]*

Amal.   There you are. Come here, Fakir, by my bedside.

Madhav.   Upon my word, but this is--

Gaffer.   *[Winking hard]* I am the fakir.

Madhav.   It beats my reckoning what you're not.

Amal.   Where have you been this time, Fakir?

Fakir.   To the Isle of Parrots. I am just back.

Madhav.   The Parrots' Isle!

Fakir.   Is it so very astonishing? Am I like you, man? A journey doesn't cost a thing. I tramp just where I like.

Amal.   *[Clapping]* How jolly for you! Remember your promise

	to take me with you as your follower when I'm well.
Fakir.	Of course, and I'll teach you such secrets too of travelling that nothing in sea or forest or mountain can bar your way.
Madhav.	What's all this rigmarole?
Gaffer.	Amal, my dear, I bow to nothing in sea or mountain; but if the doctor joins in with this uncle of yours, then I with all my magic must own myself beaten.
Amal.	No. Uncle shan't tell the doctor. And I promise to lie quiet; but the day I am well, off I go with the Fakir and nothing in sea or mountain or torrent shall stand in my way.
Madhav.	Fie, dear child, don't keep on harping upon going! It makes me so sad to hear you talk so.
Amal.	Tell me, Fakir, what the Parrots' Isle is like.
Gaffer.	It's a land of wonders; it's a haunt of birds. There's no man; and they neither speak nor walk, they simply sing and they fly.
Amal.	How glorious! And it's by some sea?
Gaffer.	Of course. It's on the sea.
Amal.	And green hills are there?
Gaffer.	Indeed, they live among the green hills; and in the time of the sunset when there is a red glow on the hillside, all the birds with their green wings flock back to their nests.
Amal.	And there are waterfalls!
Gaffer.	Dear me, of course; you don't have a hill without its waterfalls. Oh, it's like molten diamonds; and, my dear, what dances they have! Don't they make the pebbles sing as they rush over them to the sea. No devil of a doctor can stop them for a moment. The birds looked upon me as nothing but a man, quite a trifling creature without wings--and they would have nothing to do with me. Were it not so I would build a small cabin for myself among their crowd of nests and pass my days counting the sea waves.

Amal.	How I wish I were a bird! Then--
Gaffer.	But that would have been a bit of a job; I hear you've fixed up with the dairyman to be a hawker of curds when you grow up; I'm afraid such business won't flourish among birds; you might land yourself into serious loss.
Madhav. crazy.	Really this is too much. Between you two I shall turn Now, I'm off.
Amal.	Has the dairyman been, Uncle?
Madhav.	And why shouldn't he? He won't bother his head running errands for your pet fakir, in and out among the nests in his Parrots' Isle. But he has left a jar of curd for you saying that he is rather busy with his niece's wedding in the village, and he has got to order a band at Kamlipara.
Amal.	But he is going to marry me to his little niece.
Gaffer.	Dear me, we are in a fix now.
Amal.	He said she would find me a lovely little bride with a pair of pearl drops in her ears and dressed in a lovely red *saree*; and in the morning she would milk with her own hands the black cow and feed me with warm milk with foam on it from a brand new earthen cruse; and in the evenings she would carry the lamp round the cow-house, and then come and sit by me to tell me tales of Champa and his six brothers.
Gaffer.	How delicious! The prospect tempts even me, a hermit! But never mind, dear, about this wedding. Let it be. I tell you when you wed there'll be no lack of nieces in his household.
Madhav.	Shut up! This is more than I can stand.

[Exit]

Amal.	Fakir, now that Uncle's off, just tell me, has the King sent me a letter to the Post Office?
Gaffer.	I gather that his letter has already started; but it's still on the way.
Amal.	On the way? Where is it? Is it on that road winding

	through the trees which you can follow to the end of the forest when the sky is quite clear after rain?
Gaffer.	That's so. You know all about it already.
Amal.	I do, everything.
Gaffer.	So I see, but how?
Amal.	I can't say; but it's quite clear to me. I fancy I've seen it often in days long gone by. How long ago I can't tell. Do you know when? I can see it all: there, the King's postman coming down the hillside alone, a lantern in his left hand and on his back a bag of letters climbing down for ever so long, for days and nights, and where at the foot of the mountain the waterfall becomes a stream he takes to the footpath on the bank and walks on through the rye; then comes the sugarcane field and he disappears into the narrow lane cutting through the tall stems of sugarcanes; then he reaches the open meadow where the cricket chirps and where there is not a single man to be seen, only the snipe wagging their tails and poking at the mud with their bills. I can feel him coming nearer and nearer and my heart becomes glad.
Gaffer.	My eyes aren't young; but you make me see all the same.
Amal.	Say, Fakir, do you know the King who has this Post Office?
Gaffer.	I do; I go to him for my alms every day.
Amal.	Good! When I get well, I must have my alms too from him, mayn't I?
Gaffer.	You won't need to ask, my dear, he'll give it to you of his own accord.
Amal.	No, I would go to his gate and cry, "Victory to thee, O King!" and dancing to the tabor's sound, ask for alms. Won't it be nice?
Gaffer.	It would be splendid, and if you're with me, I shall have my full share. But what'll you ask?
Amal.	I shall say, "Make me your postman, that I may go about lantern in hand, delivering your letters from

	door to door. Don't let me stay at home all day!"
Gaffer.	What is there to be sad for, my child, even were you to stay at home?
Amal.	It isn't sad. When they shut me in here first I felt the day was so long. Since the King's Post Office I like it more and more being indoors, and as I think I shall get a letter one day, I feel quite happy and then I don't mind being quiet and alone. I wonder if I shall make out what'll be in the King's letter?
Gaffer.	Even if you didn't wouldn't it be enough if it just bore your name?

[Madhav Enters]

Madhav.	Have you any idea of the trouble you've got me into, between you two?
Gaffer.	What's the matter?
Madhav.	I hear you've let it get rumored about that the King has planted his office here to send messages to both of you.
Gaffer.	Well, what about it?
Madhav.	Our headman Panchanan has had it told to the King anonymously.
Gaffer.	Aren't we aware that everything reaches the King's ears?
Madhav.	Then why don't you look out? Why take the King's name in vain? You'll bring me to ruin if you do.
Amal.	Say, Fakir, will the King be cross?
Gaffer.	Cross, nonsense! And with a child like you and a fakir such as I am. Let's see if the King be angry, and then won't I give him a piece of my mind.
Amal.	Say, Fakir, I've been feeling a sort of darkness coming over my eyes since the morning. Everything seems like a dream. I long to be quiet. I don't feel like talking at all. Won't the King's letter come? Suppose this room melts away all on a sudden, suppose--
Gaffer.	[Fanning Amal] The letter's sure to come to-day, my boy.

[Doctor Enters]

Doctor.	And how do you feel to-day?
Amal.	Feel awfully well to-day, Doctor. All pain seems to have left me.
Doctor.	[Aside to Madhav] Don't quite like the look of that smile. Bad sign that, his feeling well! Chakradhan has observed--
Madhav.	For goodness sake, Doctor, leave Chakradhan alone. Tell me what's going to happen?
Doctor.	Can't hold him in much longer, I fear! I warned you before--This looks like a fresh exposure.
Madhav.	No, I've used the utmost care, never let him out of doors; and the windows have been shut almost all the time.
Doctor.	There's a peculiar quality in the air to-day. As I came in I found a fearful draught through your front door. That's most hurtful. Better lock it at once. Would it matter if this kept your visitors off for two or three days? If someone happens to call unexpectedly--there's the back door. You had better shut this window as well, it's letting in the sunset rays only to keep the patient awake.
Madhav.	Amal has shut his eyes. I expect he is sleeping. His face tells me--Oh, Doctor, I bring in a child who is a stranger and love him as my own, and now I suppose I must lose him!
Doctor.	What's that? There's your headman sailing in!--What a bother! I must be going, brother. You had better stir about and see to the doors being properly fastened. I will send on a strong dose directly I get home. Try it on him--it may save him at last, if he can be saved at all

[Exeunt Madhav and Doctor.]

[The Headman Enters]

Headman.	Hello, urchin!
Gaffer.	[Rising hastily] 'Sh, be quiet.
Amal.	No, Fakir, did you think I was asleep? I wasn't. I can hear everything; yes, and voices far away. I feel that

mother and father are sitting by my pillow and speaking to me.

[Madhav Enters]

Headman.	I say, Madhav, I hear you hobnob with bigwigs nowadays.
Madhav.	Spare me your jests, Headman, we are but common people.
Headman.	But your child here is expecting a letter from the King.
Madhav.	Don't you take any notice of him, a mere foolish boy!
Headman.	Indeed, why not! It'll beat the King hard to find a better family! Don't you see why the King plants his new Post Office right before your win- dow? Why there's a letter for you from the King, urchin.
Amal.	[Starting up] Indeed, really!
Headman.	How can it be false? You're the King's chum. Here's your letter [showing a blank slip of paper]. Ha, ha, ha! This is the letter.
Amal.	Please don't mock me. Say, Fakir, is it so?
Gaffer.	Yes, my dear. I as Fakir tell you it is his letter.
Amal.	How is it I can't see? It all looks so blank to me. What is there in the letter, Mr. Headman?
Headman.	The King says, "I am calling on you shortly; you had better arrange puffed rice offerings for me.--Palace fare is quite tasteless to me now." Ha! ha! ha!
Madhav.	[With folded palms] I beseech you, headman, don't you joke about these things--
Gaffer.	Cutting jokes indeed, dare he!
Madhav.	Are you out of your mind too, Gaffer?
Gaffer.	Out of my mind, well then I am; I can read plainly that the King writes he will come himself to see Amal, with the state physician.
Amal.	Fakir, Fakir, 'sh, his trumpet! Can't you hear?
Headman.	Ha! ha! ha! I fear he won't until he's a bit more off his head.
Amal.	Mr. Headman, I thought you were cross with me and didn't love me. I never could think you would fetch me

	the King's letter. Let me wipe the dust off your feet.
Headman.	This little child does have an instinct of reverence. Though a little silly, he has a good heart.
Amal.	It's hard on the fourth watch now, I suppose--Hark the gong, "Dong, dong, ding," "Dong, dong, ding." Is the evening star up? How is it I can't see--
Gaffer.	Oh, the windows are all shut, I'll open them.

[A knocking outside]

Madhav.	What's that?--Who is it--what a bother!
	Voice [From outside] Open the door.
Madhav.	Say, Headman--Hope they're not robbers.
Headman.	Who's there?--It's Panchanan, the headman, calls--Aren't you afraid of the like of me? Fancy! The noise has ceased! Panchanan's voice carries far.--Yes, show me the biggest robbers!
Madhav.	[Peering out of the window] I should think the noise has ceased. They've smashed the door.
	[The King's Herald enters]
Herald.	Our Sovereign King comes to-night!
Headman.	My God!
Amal.	At what hour of the night, Herald?
Herald.	On the second watch.
Amal.	When from the city gates my friend the watchman will strike his gong, "ding dong ding, ding dong ding"--then?
Herald.	Yes, then. The King sends his greatest physician to attend on his young friend.

[State Physician Enters]

Physician.	What's this? How close it is here! Open wide all the doors and windows. [Feeling Amal's body] How do you feel, my child?
Amal.	I feel very well, Doctor, very well. All pain is gone. How fresh and open! I can see all the stars now twinkling from the other side of the dark.
Physician.	Will you feel well enough to leave your bed with the King when he comes in the middle watches of the night?

Amal.	Of course, I'm dying to be about for ever so long. I'll ask the King to find me the polar star.--I must have seen it often, but I don't know exactly which it is.
Physician.	He will tell you everything. [To Madhav] Will you go about and arrange flowers through the room for the King's visit? [Indicating the Headman] We can't have that person in here.
Amal.	No, let him be, Doctor. He is a friend. It was he who brought me the King's letter.
Physician.	Very well, my child. He may remain if he is a friend of yours.
Madhav.	[Whispering into Amal's ear] My child, the King loves you. He is coming himself. Beg for a gift from him. You know our humble circumstances.
Amal.	Don't you worry, Uncle.--I've made up my mind about it.
Madhav.	What is it, my child?
Amal.	I shall ask him to make me one of his postmen that I may wander far and wide, delivering his message from door to door.
Madhav.	[Slapping his forehead] Alas, is that all?
Amal.	What'll be our offerings to the King, Uncle, when he comes?
Herald.	He has commanded puffed rice.
Amal.	Puffed rice! Say, Headman, you're right. You said so. You knew all we didn't.
Headman.	If you send word to my house then I could manage for the King's advent really nice--
Physician.	No need at all. Now be quiet all of you. Sleep is coming over him. I'll sit by his pillow; he's dropping into slumber. Blow out the oil-lamp. Only let the star-light stream in. Hush, he slumbers.
Madhav.	[Addressing Gaffer] What are you standing there for like a statue, folding your palms.--I am nervous.--Say, are they good omens? Why are they darkening the room? How will star-light help?

Gaffer.	Silence, unbeliever.

[Sudha Enters]

Sudha.	Amal!
Physician.	He's asleep.
Sudha.	I have some flowers for him. Mayn't I give them into his own hand?
Physician.	Yes, you may.
Sudha.	When will he be awake?
Physician.	Directly the King comes and calls him.
Sudha.	Will you whisper a word for me in his ear?
Physician.	What shall I say?
Sudha.	Tell him Sudha has not forgotten him.

Curtain